ECLIPSED SUNSHINE

A DARK ROMANCE NOVEL

D.W. MARSHALL

To my husband for being my best friend.

I love you.

1

WHITNEY

"*A*re you sure it's not too much?" I ask about my new dress, *and* the makeup, *and* the fancy hair. To be honest, I feel like a doll being dressed up, and if I'm being *really* honest, this whole charade reminds of the place I don't want to speak about.

All this fuss over me, ensuring that not a hair is out of place, so that I'm the perfect play toy. I don't want to go back there in my body or mind, but too many little things remind me of the worst year of my entire life. Nothing matters though, I've been home for three weeks and most nights I wake up in a cold sweat from a dream so real that it takes an eternity before I realize I am home—I am free.

It could be something as simple as a smell that drifts through the air that brings me back to that awful room with the obnoxiously cheery yellow décor, the oversized bed fit for a queen, and the location of my worst imaginings. And somehow being home, standing here with my two best gals as they pretty me up for dinner with Thomas feels no different. In fact, it's much worse. I feel like a fraud for trying to forget what happened to me—that the last year was something I made up. My friend's think tonight is the night that Thomas is going to propose to me, just like they were so sure he was going to before I was taken. But, why would someone like me think that I deserve a happy ending, when I'm so obviously cursed?

Who am I kidding? I stare into the mirror at my reflection. Gone is the fresh-faced girl with the light brown complexion that looked at the world with hope and optimism. I fear I will never be her again.

"This is a bad idea." I pull the earrings off, grab a tissue and start wiping off the lipstick. Nothing about any of this feels right to me.

I shouldn't be doing anything but crawling into my bed. I'm always so tired. My gals don't get it, and I don't expect them to. Unless they've been where I've been, they can't.

In The Chamber my life was not my own. My body belonged to someone else. An entire year can't be erased with pretty dresses and fancy dinners. Makeup can't cover up the truth. My friends don't have horrid images burned into their memories. Their faith in humanity isn't shattered.

When they look at me I know they see a young woman who has a full life ahead of her, who should be ready to face it with a grateful smile. They can't possibly understand that I'm not that young woman anymore. She isn't inside of me. I don't feel her in my rigid smile. My heart that used to beat with excitement and joy, now only beats to sustain my life—I can't even manage to conjure up enough hope, not even for tonight. I long for butterflies in the pit of my stomach and daydreams about the future.

Chalice and Amaris had the best intentions for tonight, but if they knew what I suffered, they would know that everything about tonight reminds me of that place, my lost year.

Spending hours getting dolled up for a man is the last thing I want to do. But, one look at my friends and I can see it in their eyes—hope. They stand and watch me with hope that I'm okay, hope that things can return to normal for me and for them. They don't want me to be stuck, and I get it, neither does my mom, or my dad, or Thomas. But they aren't giving me time.

"Stop. What are you doing?" Amaris says, her warm island accent soothing, even in frustration, as she runs at me to grab the tissue from my hand. "I put a lot of work into making you look like heaven and you're wiping it all to hell."

I flop onto the edge of my bed. I can't tell them I don't want to go out. When Thomas set tonight up, I *was* excited. The idea that he has welcomed me back into his arms knowing everything I've been through is an answered prayer. And when my gals and I went dress shopping yesterday I was floating on a puffy cloud. Grateful that after everything I'd suffered I can come home and have all of this, this, normal. The icing on the cake is a date with the man whose love helped me survive my year in captivity. Maybe, I've been lying to myself, and I do deserve a happy ending.

Last night, I stared at my little green dress and imagined sitting across from Thomas and his amazing smile. I envisioned him proposing and of course, me saying yes. Thoughts of how tonight would go kept me up all night, and let's be honest, it was much better than the thoughts that normally plague me.

"I can't do this. I need to call and cancel. I'm really tired."

"Don't be foolish. You have to move on with your life, sweets. Thomas waited a whole year for you. How long do you think he will continue to wait?" Chalice asks.

I shrug my shoulders. I have no idea how long. I know if I loved someone I wouldn't implement a time limit, and I would want them at their best. I certainly wouldn't rush them after something so traumatic, but that's me. Maybe three weeks is long enough. I mean, I don't want to lose him. What Chalice is saying is harsh but true, and I'm smart enough to know that everyone will scatter if I continue to walk around with a dark cloud over my head. What else can I do? Three weeks is all they've given me.

Ignoring all the contrary feelings coursing through me, I glance around and note that this is my bedroom, not the yellow room that haunts me. In fact, there isn't a stitch of yellow in sight. My room is so different than *that* place. Thankfully.

Missing are the elaborate and ornate furnishings, the sex toys, a bed big enough for four. Gone is the groomer who tended to all my needs. In its place my best gal friends who love me and everything that is, or was, simply me.

"You're right. I have to try." I hand Amaris the tube of lipstick and she begins reapplying. While she goes to work, I think about my Thomas. We have been spending a lot of time together in the weeks that I've been home. He is everything that I remembered him to be—kind, patient, and loving. Having him to come home to lessens some of the pain from the last year. I can do this for him and for us. And if I'm lucky, tonight will be the night I dreamed it would be, the night that was stolen from me a year ago.

I stand up, walk over to the mirror and gaze at myself. It takes every-thing for me to not feel like I'm preparing for an entirely different night. "Thomas said dress to impress," I say in a soft voice.

"And you, my dear, are dazzling," Amaris says.

Okay, Whitney, you can do this. You are not locked away in a gothic castle. You are home in your beloved Barbados. The sun is always shining, and you are free, I say to myself as I stare at my reflection.

Amaris could work in The Chamber, she's that good. I shake my head to douse the errant thought.

My makeup is natural, just like I like it. My green dress shouts spring glamour. The hem rests about a foot above my knee and the dress clings to my curves. I feel naked. Since I've been home, I have avoided anything that makes me sexy. Baggy and loose has been my modus operandi. Standing here in this dress, I feel almost Chamber ready, and I hate myself for it. My heart is hammering in my chest and my stomach is queasy.

"What's wrong?" Chalice asks.

I don't answer her. The lump in my throat makes it hard for me to speak. When the tears spring forth from my eyes, I crawl onto my bed. My gals share the silence with me and climb onto the bed. "I don't think I can leave the house dressed like this."

"You look beautiful," Chalice says with a question in her voice.

"That's just it. I don't want to look that way," I admit.

My friends don't say anything, but I know them well and they want to.

"I know it sounds insane. But the man who took me said he loved to collect beautiful play things. Maybe if I didn't wear sexy things he would have never noticed me."

They squeeze me tighter. "How can that be true? I'm much sexier than you, sweets, and he didn't take me," Chalice teases, and it's just what I need because I burst into laughter wilted with tears.

"Seriously, though. If you change every part of who you are because of that evil monster, then you're letting him win. He already took so much from you. You can't let him have it all," Amaris says.

I nod; she's right. That's one of the things my therapist has been telling me in both my group and private sessions, and it feels right to hear it. Sometimes I feel like I'm on the path to getting back to the old me, and I want it, I need it. But then other times, when I'm not in the company of my therapist or fellow trauma survivors, it's an entirely different scenario. When my friends and family are with me, I feel so different, not like myself at all, and what's worse is they all look at me differently too. I don't think they do it on purpose; I don't think they can help themselves. Around them, I'm bare. I don't feel empowered. I don't feel strong, and I'm afraid all the time.

What if he takes me again? What if someone else does the same thing? How can I be me again? The old me? That girl is so far gone I wouldn't know her if she was standing right in front of me.

"I'll try."

The three of us sit up in my bed and share a group hug.

"I love you guys."

"We love you, too."

Amaris wipes my tears. "We're here for you, and we'll help you through this, okay?"

I nod my head and smile. But her words make the tears fall harder. I know I'm too emotional for all of this, but Thomas is so worth me trying.

"You'll be safe tonight. Thomas is tough. If there are any bad guys out there, he won't let them near you, sweets," Chalice says.

My friends are right about Thomas; he loves me and I know he can keep me safe. He has been taking things slow with me, not to the point of treating me like glass, but close. I have been as honest and transparent about what I suffered as I can.

As much as I want to forget, Thomas won't let me; he says I need to speak about it so that I can heal. As resistant as I am, my therapist says he's right and if he is someone that I can trust and open up to, it will only help me in my healing process.

Recently, Thomas confided in me about his own struggles. I think it's his way of showing his vulnerability to me. Thomas is a very proud and shrewd business man, so him trusting me with the knowledge of his recent financial woes and unemployment had to be very hard on him. He has never made our time together about him, but his honesty has made confiding in him easier—a little. He is attentive to me and my needs and promises me that we will both be okay. But I can't help but feel responsible for what he has lost. He has never come out and said that it was my fault that he lost so much, but in some way, I have to believe if I hadn't been kidnapped he'd probably be as successful as he was before I left. I can only imagine how hard it was for him while I was missing.

I almost told him about the money twice. Knowing about the four million dollars I received from Mason wouldn't just lift his mood, he could actually bounce back and return to the amazing business career he had before.

But I haven't told him; I haven't told anyone.

Even when I think I might be able to, I can't fix my mouth to say the words. Knowing how much I could help the people that I love makes me feel even more guilty for keeping this to myself. But to speak it makes what happened to me more than real.

The money makes me feel dirty.

When I do get the courage to tell him, I hope he is happy and doesn't look at me differently. This is the man I hope to spend the rest of my life with, and I plan to do everything in my power to help him—I just need to tell him when I'm ready and that isn't right now.

"Come with me," Amaris says and pulls me to stand. She sets me in the chair in front of my mirror.

She goes to work fixing my makeup. "You can do this. You deserve to look beautiful for your fiancé," Amaris says.

"He isn't my fiancé, Amaris."

"He will be after tonight, sweets," Chalice says and mists me with body spray.

I roll my eyes at them both. "I wouldn't be so sure," I say under my breath.

The doorbell rings just as Amaris finishes retouching my makeup. My stomach hits the floor.

Daddy knocks on the door and pokes his head in. "Baby, Thomas is here. You ready?"

I slip on my matching heels and follow my dad out of my bedroom door and down the hall, my girls on my heels.

"Baby, you look beautiful," Daddy says.

"Thanks, Daddy. I wish Mom was here."

He shakes his head. "She does, too. She hated leaving when you just got home. But she called today and said your grandmother is doing much better, so she will be home before you know it," he promises and gives me a kiss on my forehead.

Thomas stands up from the sofa to greet me. He is stunning. His dark brown skin looks divine in his ocean blue suit that is tailor-made for him. "Wow, Whitney. You take my breath away," he says and takes the short steps to me. He acknowledges my gals and reaches his hand out for me. I take it. *Can he feel how moist my palms are?* If he does, he's too much of a gentleman to react to it.

"Thomas, take care of my baby," Daddy says.

"Yes, sir, I will."

2

THE CHAMBER, WEEK ONE

"*A*re you ready for tonight?" I ask Violet.

She shakes her head. "I don't think it's possible. Are you?"

I let out a long sigh and take a seat next to her on her bed. The way she has her red hair tied in a high ponytail, revealing fresh freckled skin make her appear much too young to be in a place like this. Not that my twenty years qualifies me. No person should be subjected to this horror.

Violet and I are roommates in this horrible place. It's only been a week since we were brought here. A lot has happened, but tonight is the big night. Our first night with the men in our individual rooms. My stomach churns thinking about it.

"I'm scared to death. Literally shaking." I hold my hand up and show her the tremor that has been with me since I was taken. "I don't think I can do this."

She wraps her arms around me and I copy the action. We sit in silence holding one another, comforting each other in our time of need, we both sob.

"Sunshine." A voice I am already too familiar with calls from the door.

I look up and find Layne, my groomer, standing there. I squeeze Violet. "Are we sure it's too late to try to break out?" I whisper into her ear.

"Where would we go?" she asks.

"At least we're not alone. I'll say a prayer for you," I say.

"Me too," she says.

"Iris should be along any minute for you, Violet," Layne says. If we were anywhere else her smile would be comforting. She is a beautiful woman, with long light brown hair, a lithe body, and bright green eyes. But she works here; she is one of them. According to Mason, our groomers are supposed to be our right-hand person in this place. The way I see it, if you work here, you can't be trusted.

I follow Layne through the zigzagging halls. When we arrive at the spa Flame, Sky, and Raven are already there. We offer each other smiles that were meant to comfort, but instead relay our fears. Within a few minutes the room fills with all seven of us, and our groomers. We sit in salon chairs, while the groomers, poke and prod, smooth and tweeze. Lane reclines my chair and instructs me to flip over onto my stomach. She gives me the most amazing massage I have ever had.

I feel a hand graze my skin. I raise my hand in search of the touch and grasp the hand of the person next to me—Sky.

Tears spill from my eyes and hit the floor below me. I can't believe this is my life.

"Ladies. Ladies. It's time!" Mason's deep voice breaks through the silence.

Layne steps away from me, and I sit up on the edge of my seat. I lock eyes with Mason, for a brief second, before his gaze slides down to admire each of us. A smile on his face—pride. A cold shiver shoots through my body.

"We have no time to waste. The lucky winners are already here waiting. Make me proud," he says, then turns on his heel and walks out."

None of us says a word, but the energy is palpable—fear.

Layne sits next to me. "We have to go. I still need to get you dressed."

Like a doll that isn't capable of dressing itself, I follow her back through the maze and into my chamber—yellow everywhere, so much yellow. On the bed, on the walls. Not the furniture, that's dark wood. I follow Layne to my chamber bathroom. She makes fast work of sweeping my hair into a messy updo, and I step into a sleek yellow gown that is completely sheer, held together by two ties that are like nooses against my skin.

"Beautiful," Layne says.

"Montreal is at the bottom of the stairs, should you need anything. Good luck."

Layne slips away, leaving me alone. Before I have a chance to panic, a man is standing in the doorway—my first visitor for the night.

"Sunshine, you are dazzling," he says. The man stalks forward. He is tall, well over six feet with deep olive-skin, and a muscular build. I stay put as he crosses the room to me. While I do my best to control my breathing—even still my head swirls and gets light. Passing out would be the best and worst thing for me to do right now.

I've had sex before. I have a boyfriend, had a boyfriend. But never like this, against my will. Prettied up like a doll for this man, and the many others waiting their turn.

"Call me, Connell."

He is so close to me. His hand grazes my arm, leaving cold in its wake. "I've put my name in the hat for two years to get a coveted spot in

Mason's fuck-fest. I plan to make every second memorable, starting with you. His lips are on mine, at first gentle, almost sweet. I kiss him back, afraid of what would happen if I chose instead to stand mannequin still.

"Yes, Sunshine." He breathes into my mouth as he undoes the bottom tie.

My breath catches in my throat. Tremors rattle through me. My dress gathers into a puddle on the floor between us. My mind goes to my family, Thomas. I will never survive this, but I have to. He steps back and stares at me. He motions for me to spin around and my stomach rolls with nausea when he whistles his appreciation.

"Fucking splendid," he says and cups one of my breasts in his hand and begins licking and slurping my nipple. "Are you wet for me?" he asks and plunges an unknown number of fingers deep inside me. "Fuck yeah you are."

Tears begin pooling in my eyes, and I tip my head back trying to coax them back to where they came from—epic fail. Instead they roll down the sides of my face. I swipe them quick and pretend to have brought my arms up to play in his hair.

"You like that?" he asks.

"Yes." I lie. My heart is pounding through my chest.

I gasp when he picks me up. He holds onto my ass and tosses me onto the bed. He stares down at me, his chest rising and falling as he stares down at me. More tears invade, and I don't attempt to wipe them.

"Don't be afraid, love. Sex is a beautiful thing. Time has made it into something more intimate and personal." He watches me as he unbuttons his shirt, slow and deliberate, never taking his eyes off me.

I fight the sobs that want to break through.

"Animals in nature don't need to court each other. A dog can walk up to another dog on the street, fuck it senseless and go about its day.

Humans assigned labels to sex. When it is primal and organic, it's like an addictive drug."

His shirt falls to the floor. He is as strong as he looked clothed. A chest and abdomen that is rippled with muscles, not bulky, but tight and hard. Dark hair lightly covers his chest and trails down his stomach. I tear my eyes from his body when his hands go for his belt.

"I won't be gentle, but I promise to leave you wanting so much more."

When his pants hit the floor, my body shakes more. But I don't have much time to contemplate my immediate future. He falls forward in a swift motion and sinks his cock inside of me. My eyes widen to double their size with the fullness of him. He watches me, as he pulls out of me and slams back inside of me, over and over. My body takes over despite my fight for it not to do so. Traitorous moans escape me, my back arches wanting more.

"Feel it, Sunshine."

He pushes deep inside of me and stays there this time, moving his hips in circles, punishing me with his fullness. I match his motions until I come apart, my body slamming into his and pushing so hard my bones ache. I shake and shutter, and yell out.

"My turn," he says and flips me over onto my stomach, pulling me onto my knees.

He grabs onto my ass and pulls until my back is arched in the extreme. "I am going to fuck you so hard you'll dream about me." He pushes inside me, slower this time. Moaning as he does it. Then he raises my legs off the bed. While holding onto them, he picks up speed, pumping his cock inside of me with desperation, until he shouts and squeezes my skin, filling me with his essence.

I collapse onto the bed, and he falls next to me.

"What do you think? Carnal. Not scary?"

I don't say what I'm thinking, which is: yes, it would be if I met you at a club and made the decision to do this with you. "Still scary, but you made it less scary. Yes, carnal."

He runs his fingers through my hair. Unexpected.

"We are going to be spending a lot of time together. In time it won't be scary at all, I promise. Thank you for being my first."

My eyes get big. *His first?*

"Chambermaid, I mean."

He kisses me on the lips, grabs his clothes and leaves.

3

*T*he restaurant is gorgeous—the kind of place you spend hours getting dressed up for—located inside of the lavish Crane Beach Hotel that sits near the water.

Thomas leans forward and says to the host. "Reservation for two under Thomas Ackerly." The man scans a tablet for our reservation. Thomas oozes power and confidence. No one would ever guess at him having money problems. Maybe my gals were right and he is planning a romantic proposal. Otherwise, why would a man with money problems bring his girlfriend to such an expensive restaurant. "I requested a table near the window overlooking the ocean," he continues.

"Yes, sir. I believe your table is ready."

I fidget when the host smiles and stares at me too long. Thrusting me back into my uncomfortable place. Thomas pulls me closer to him. He feels it too.

The gentleman takes us to our table and like Thomas requested, we are seated along a series of windows overlooking the water. "Beautiful," I say. I can only imagine how amazing the view will be when the sun sets. Thomas pulls my seat out for me.

Wow, he makes me feel special.

"Good evening, and welcome to L'Azure," a waitress says, her islander accent like a soothing song. The two of us look up. "Would you like to start with a drink?"

Thomas clears his throat. "Your best champagne," he says.

I watch him as he commands attention. He has always had this powerful presence, as if he is leagues more important in status than he is. I know that's one reason he brought me here, even when he and I both know this place is too expensive. He knows his worth. Which is why he has always been so successful in business, and another reason that I believe in my heart that he will land on his feet and bounce back quickly. I hope the same for myself.

When the waitress leaves, I brace myself to say what's on my mind. "Thomas, I know you want to make tonight special, but maybe you shouldn't spend so much money. I'd be fine with a lot less—" I glance around the room, "—extravagance."

Thomas slides his hand over mine. "Darling, everything is fine. I've got an amazing deal in the works that will change everything." His smile is dazzling.

This news cheers me up. I have too much in my life to feel guilty for, and Thomas' career getting back on track would take one thing off my heavily loaded plate. "That's fantastic news, Thomas. You deserve all the success."

He flashes me a dashing smile before saying, "*We* deserve it."

A man comes to our table with champagne and two glasses. He opens the bottle, fills our glasses with flair, leaving the bottle.

"Whitney, a year ago when you went missing, I went crazy. I was lost without you. I didn't care about my business or anything else, just finding you." He raises his glass. But I don't join him in the action. The lump finds my throat again and it takes everything in my body not to cry. I risk ruining such a beautiful night by turning into a slobbering baby.

"I'm sorry for what you lost," I manage to say to him.

He takes my hand and sets his glass down.

"Nothing to be sorry about. I'm resilient, and now that you're home I feel like I can do anything. This is a cause for celebration, not tears, eh." He picks up his glass again and gestures for me to pick up mine, and I do. "To the love of my life coming back to me," he says, and we both take a drink. The champagne is refreshing and the perfect amount of sweet. Delicious. My eyes catch the familiar little blue velvet box as Thomas places it on the table.

I gasp. "Thomas." I set my glass down and look at him, stunned. He is so good-looking and confident. The kind of guy most parents dream of their daughter finding. Handsome, strong, intelligent. I count myself as lucky enough to be sitting opposite this man that still wants me.

Thomas opens the box. The ring is stunning, but simple. A white gold band with a single solitaire, surrounded by a bouquet of three rows of smaller diamonds. "It's beautiful," I say.

He snaps the box shut. "Tonight, I plan to make all of your dreams come true. But I need a favor."

My face must bare my confusion. *What favor could possibly be tied to a proposal?* "Anything," I say.

Thomas leans forward and I mimic the action. "There's a man upstairs. A client."

I don't say anything because I have no idea what he's talking about.

Thomas gets up from his chair and moves it around the table to sit next to me. "I want us to go into business together, become a team."

"I don't understand. What kind of team?"

His smile broadens. "The client is going to pay me twenty-five hundred dollars to spend a couple of hours with you."

There is no way that I'm hearing him right. This man that I love. I know that my brain twisted what he actually said into something heart-wrenching and horrific. Because if what I think he said is in fact what he said, then my world will tip on its axis.

"I couldn't have heard you right. What is this client expecting me to do with him for a couple of hours?"

"Don't you see? This is the answer to everything. We'd be in business together. I'm not asking you to do anything you haven't done before, only this time it won't be by force. It'll be empowering now because you're choosing to do this, completely consensual, and best of all, you'll be paid. We'll be paid." His smile is wide and proud.

I sit and stare at this man I just realized I can't possibly know, not really. I have no words.

After everything I've been through, this is how he sees me? Has he always seen me this way?

I can only manage to stare at him, no, through him. The sounds in the restaurant become muffled, lost in the background. The only sound I can hear is the thudding of my heart as it pulses loudly throughout my body.

He takes my hands into his. I don't give them to him freely or pull them away; it's as though part of me isn't here anymore. My body is numb, like I'm not sitting at this table in this beautiful oceanfront restaurant, next to the man who was supposed to love me but just offered me the equivalent of a knife to my chest, piercing my heart with monstrous precision.

Nothing in my year-long captivity could have prepared me for this moment. Dreaming of reuniting with Thomas gave me hope and strength in my darkest time. I believed he could save me from my nightmares. I could have never prepared myself for this reality...he is my nightmare.

Even as the tears roll down my cheeks, the excitement in his voice never wanes.

Ignoring my reaction, he continues, "I've given this a lot of thought. If you spend ten hours a week working we'd clean up, twenty-five thousand a week, a hundred thousand a month. Eventually, we'll hire more women and you can sit back and collect money. What do you think?"

I snatch my hand from his as if it were on fire. I swallow hard and stare.

He is Mason.

Is this how monsters begin? It's like all the superhero movies. Some characters get their powers and immediately do good, I guess because good is inside of them. While others turn to the dark side and want to hurt people, conquer or rule the world. Obviously, the darkness was always inside of them. And here I sit, next to the man I thought I loved, and I'm seeing him for the first time. Thomas is shrouded in darkness. But I still love him—it's not that easy to turn love off.

I wipe my face with the back of my hands. They shake as I bring them up to my face. When I look into his eyes they are alight and expectant. He is so sure of his plan. The background noises return and I glance around at the patrons of this beautiful establishment. I'd bet all the money Mason paid me that none of the other women here have boyfriends that believe they are whores. I could simply stand up and walk away. I'm sure Daddy could be here in less than twenty minutes, and the second I tell him what Thomas wants his precious youngest daughter to do he would promptly kick his ass. I stare at the rolling sea, I give attention to the wait staff bustling around, anything but the monster at my table. After eons pass, I finally turn my attention to Thomas, and try to appeal to his senses.

"What you're asking me to do is illegal."

He scoots closer to me, taking his hand and running it up and down my thigh. A motion twenty minutes ago I would have counted as romantic, but now, is making my skin crawl.

"We'll be discrete, only top tier clientele, and we don't have to do this forever, just until I get on my feet," he says.

I look down at the table. The tears come back. I couldn't stop them if I wanted to. My heart physically hurts from beating so hard and fast. My stomach is in knots. Come to think of it my head hurts too, the pain slamming against my skull. This is what I couldn't wait to come back to? Is this how everyone sees me? My family? My friends? After everything I went through, this is what I've been reduced to?

"Why are you so upset, eh?" he has the nerve to ask.

It takes everything I have not to shout, create a scene. "Are you serious? You thought I'd love this idea? Did you think I enjoyed my time being passed around from man to man? I was kidnapped, Thomas. I didn't join some sex club." I throw my hands to my face and take deep breaths before continuing. "You thought I'd come home and jump at the chance to screw the entire island?" I pause, trying to catch my breath. "I'm seeing a therapist because of what happened to me. I'm in a trauma survivors group, Thomas. I have nightmares, almost every night."

I stare at him with pleading eyes. I need him to see me differently, to love me the way I imagined he would. I beg him to be the man I came home for.

"Can you do this for me? For us?" he asks, ignoring everything I just said.

My attention switches focus from his eyes, and drifts across the table to the little blue box. I can't believe how excited I was moments ago. The box held with it the promise of love and happily ever after. Now I realize it is only the start of a dark and twisted fairytale, where nothing but heartache happens in the end. Why did I think I deserved more?

A heavy sigh escapes me. I am mentally exhausted. If the man who is supposed to love me sees me this way, maybe this is all that I am, all that I have left. A chambermaid forever. I look up at Thomas, into his hopeful eyes. "I'll do it."

Thomas' face registers surprise. "Really?" He beams. "You've made me the happiest man alive. I can't wait to marry you." He kisses me on the lips. It isn't sweet or gentle. He slides me a room key, wasting no time.

Wow, I don't even get dinner.

"He's waiting for you upstairs. Baby, thank you. This is the start of something big."

I'm sick to my stomach. I stand on shaky legs, reach for my champagne glass and down it, pour another and down it. I take the room key in my hand and start to walk away.

Thomas grabs my hand. "Baby, I love you."

I don't respond. The champagne is hitting me and I need it right now. I walk away. When I'm almost out of the restaurant, I glance back at Thomas to watch as he orders from the menu. My stomach heaves a couple of times, and it's all that I can do to make it to the ladies' room to deposit what little I have in my stomach. I stand in front of the mirror, rinse my mouth out and stare at my reflection. My hazel eyes look like Christmas, sharing the space with the red that has clouded them from crying.

I can't believe I held hope for coming home to him. How could I have been so stupid to think he was worth coming home to? He doesn't love me. He never did. If I give him this we will never be together, I know that. And even if we made it through this nightmare, will I even want him? I don't know if I want him now.

But what if he's the best that I deserve? What if no one else wants me but him? I'm all used up, what do I expect? How do you tell someone that you spent a year locked away, being passed around by thirty-five different men? No regular, normal guy is going to want me after all the hell I went through.

"Maybe crazy deserves crazy," I say to my reflection. At least I wouldn't be alone. I splash water on my face taking care not to wet my hair. I grab the room key from the counter and head up to the sixth floor.

4

WHITNEY

I take a couple of deep breaths before sliding the key card into the slot. I jump as the lock makes the familiar click. I depress the handle and push the door open and walk inside. My breathing picks up and my heart hammers inside of my chest when I scan the room and spot the man sitting at a round table having a drink. I don't move. I can't go forward into the room, nor can I retreat. My legs simply won't work. The man turns his head toward me and we are locked into an intense stare.

He is wearing a crisp deep blue dress shirt and a grey tie. My eyes leave his and scan the room. His jacket is hung across a chair. Everything is in slow motion. The room isn't yellow, but it may as well be. I may not be locked away in captivity, but he is a customer, one of the thirty-five that I had the *pleasure* to spend a year with. I throw up in my mouth and my body is wracked with chills. The man continues to regard me without saying anything.

After a long silence and me standing in the center of the room, petrified, he finally speaks. "You must be Whitney?" he asks in an accent that suggests a lot of time in America.

I am unable to find my voice.

The man is older than me, most likely in his thirties. He is extremely handsome with fair skin, chocolate hair, and he certainly doesn't look like the sort that would need to pay for sex.

"Please sit," he says.

I chance that my legs will hold me up and take cautious steps toward the table—toward him.

"I am Whitney." My voice is shaky, but I don't take my eyes from his, and I don't take a seat.

"Promise I won't bite. Please." He gestures toward the chair across from him.

This time I move toward the chair. It makes an ugly sound as it drags across the wooden floor. Time slows as I take my seat across the table from him.

The stranger and I don't speak. Instead, we only regard one another. When I was released from The Chamber three weeks ago the last place I expected to be was seated across the table from another man that expects me to hand my body to him. Worse, Thomas is downstairs waiting for this to happen, telling me that I am worthless in his eyes. To him, I never left The Chamber.

The longer I stare at this man, this stranger, the more shallow my breaths become. The faster my heart beats. My body shivers beyond my control. There is no way that I am having sex with this man. I finally speak up. "You don't look like the type of man that...I mean, you don't seem the type for this sort of thing either."

He laughs. "You're right about that. I'm just doing a favor for a friend."

I furrow my eyebrows at his comment. "You mean Thomas?"

He nods. "Thomas and I met about seven months ago. He made some risky business moves that went south. So, let's just say that I'm helping out a friend who's starting a new venture."

"By paying to sleep with me?" I maintain eye contact, while I wonder exactly how long my heart can continue to race in fear before I need emergency medical care.

"Yes," he says.

"*But*, you're only doing this for Thomas, not because this is something you normally do?"

"Yes," he says. He hitches a brow in curiosity.

I seize the opportunity. "So, can we just say we did it and that you were satisfied?"

He laughs.

I press on. Because if he is telling the truth he may agree to this. "I only ask because I'd really rather die than do this, but I'm also afraid to go back downstairs to my fiancé if I don't."

He doesn't speak. His lips are pressed into a hard line. He is considering my new proposal. "Listen, I'm a nice guy, but as a business man I'm all about transactions, goods and services." He pauses. "Wait, you said fiancé?"

"Yes," I say and nod. The words bring with them new tears.

The stranger looks away from me while he processes what I've said. Then he pulls his shoulders back and returns his gaze to mine. "Look, I feel bad that you have such a shitty fiancé, but what do I get out of this? Besides being out twenty-five hundred dollars?"

I glance down at my hands, my mind going a million miles per minute. "That's. Understandable."

He lets out a sigh. "Can I ask you a question?"

I look at him and nod.

"Why would Thomas think you'd do this for him? The guy is a tool for sure. But I'm curious why he would even think you'd be an option. Your obviously not a pro; you're scared to death." His face softens and is marred with concern.

My thoughts go to his question even though they don't have to, because I know the answer. Here is my opportunity. "Thomas and I were together when I was kidnapped a year ago and did stuff like *this*." I inhale a large amount of air and let it out. *My shame.* "Against my will. I was released about three weeks ago." I pause, searching for a rational excuse. "I guess Thomas saw an opportunity." I sigh around the last word because I can't believe what has happened. Before this moment, I thought my luck was changing. Mason kept his word and released me and the other six other girls that were held with me. I thought Thomas wanted me. I guess my luck ran out, because it seems I've jumped from the frying pan into a hellish fire. I know Thomas is that hellish fire and *his* wardrobe comes with a red smoking jacket, pitchfork, and two deadly horns growing from his head. Thomas may be sicker than Mason because Thomas actually believes he loves me.

He sits back against his chair. "Fuck me. Your boyfriend needs his ass kicked. I'd be willing to take care of that for you."

I shake my head. "Thanks, but no thanks. I don't want anyone getting hurt because of me."

"Well, I definitely can't do this shit now."

We sit and stare at each other when an idea hits me. "What if I paid you double to say you did and that it was amazing? That way you'd get something out of the deal."

He considers what I've proposed. "That gets you out of *this*, but what about the next time? I think Thomas is desperate, and once he gets his hands on this money he won't let you go so easily. Maybe you should cut your losses now," he says.

I consider his advice. "This is the best way for me right now."

"You still love him."

I nod. "Pathetic, I know."

He sighs. "Not after what you've been through. I get it, you're grasping onto whatever you can." His smile is brittle. He pities my weakness. "I'll do it, but how are you gonna get your hands on that kind of cash? We're talking seventy-five hundred dollars, 'cause Thomas is gonna be looking to get paid."

I look into this man's kind eyes, a stranger who is treating me better than the man I love. "I can wire it to you. It's part of my scholarship money. I can wire it to your account for say, security services and you give me the money to give to Thomas."

We shake hands on our deal, not exactly illegal, and for a moment, I am so thankful for this kind stranger.

"We have some time to kill," he says.

"It would seem that way."

"You mentioned scholarship money. Are you a student?"

I sit back in my seat, considerably more relaxed than when I first came. "I'm known as a genius around here. I received my Bachelor's degree at sixteen, double Master's degrees at eighteen. I took a break after that and was scheduled to attend University College in London for my Doctorate, but I was taken months before."

He looks at me as if seeing me for the first time. Obviously reassessing. I'm not unaccustomed to that look; it often follows someone learning that a black woman as young as me has accomplished so much. "How old are you?"

"Twenty-one."

"Remarkable."

I smirk. "Somehow I feel less than remarkable."

We chat for a while before the man slides an envelope across the table toward me. It's time to go, and suddenly I feel much safer in the company of this stranger. I take the envelope. I don't open it and slide it into my small purse. I stand from my seat. "Thank you. I am grateful for your kindness."

He shrugs. "It's the least I could do. Can I give you a piece of unsolicited advice?"

"Sure."

"Get yourself out of this mess. Thomas' blind ambition isn't the sort of thing someone like you should be involved in."

I nod and a shiver of fear rocks my body. "Thanks again for everything," I say and head for the door.

"Hey," he stands and says. "Take this, please."

I walk back toward him and take the business card he is handing out to me. I read the information out loud. "Nikolai Andres." I look up at him, searching for the exotic features that fit his name. The room is dimly lit, but I can see subtle exotic features in the cut of his jaw and the straightness of his nose. "Personal Trainer and private security," I read. I look up at him again and say, "Thanks."

He walks toward the door behind me. Standing, I can see that he is tall, over six feet. He opens the door for me to exit.

"I work with a great security team," he says, and I turn back toward him.

"They specialize in the personal type, if you should ever be in need," he continues, raising his eyebrows as if to say he believes I will be in need of security very soon.

There isn't much I can say in response. I offer him a smile. I know it doesn't reach my eyes, these days my smiles rarely do. I thought tonight was going to be the night to change my smiles, and I couldn't have been more wrong.

I place the card into my purse and turn and walk away. I never thought I'd be thankful to Mason for anything, ever. Out of all the things in the world to be grateful for, the money he gave me bought my way out of this nightmarish situation.

5

THE CHAMBER, THREE MONTHS

*M*y girls told me that it was only a matter of time before I would be summoned for my one-on-one sex session with Mason. I was hoping that the day would never come. I've been in this place for three months. I thought he'd forgotten about me. He definitely seems to have taken a liking to Sapphire. But, my wish didn't come true, because I am following Layne to his secret chamber. When my roomie got the call, she was missing in action for three days. Which meant that we all had to take on extra sexing duties in our chambers to pick up the slack, just like every other time Mason steals one of us away. I could look at it differently, if he keeps me for days, I'd only be fucking one person for days instead of several. But it's Mason. A shiver runs through me.

Three months into my sentence means three months closer to my release, if Mason is telling us the truth about letting us go after a year. Everything else he has told us has been true. We have not been harmed, we sleep in comfortable quarters. In the time I've been here I have wanted for nothing—except my release. The other women have become my friends, more like my sisters. We confide in each other, comfort each other, share our stories of life before this place. And our dreams of life after this place.

"Here we are." Layne stops in front of a large heavy door. "See you in a few days," she smiles. "Have fun," she calls as she hurries down the hall.

I knock on the door. A beautiful woman, naked stands before me. She is pale skinned, lithe, with magenta shoulder-length hair, and has large brown eyes. "I'm Pricilla. Welcome." She opens the door, and I follow her inside. The room is enormous. Three oversized-beds line a wall, ornately dressed in bright purples, greens, oranges, and red bedding and drapery. In the center of the room is a long table with enough food to feed a family of eight.

Mason is sitting at the head of the table, also naked. I assume as he isn't wearing a shirt. Two other women are sharing a spot at the table: one brown skinned, slightly darker and different in tone than my skin; the other similar in tone to the woman who let me in—both naked.

"Welcome, Sunshine. Please disrobe and have a seat at the table." Mason pats a spot next to him.

When I draw near I notice that the space in front of him is bare, save a small cushioned mat that is at least five inches thick and the same navy as the fabric covering the table. I let my robe drop to the floor and make my way to the spot he directed me to.

He hops up and pulls my chair out for me, his massive cock coming into view. He presses against my ass and kisses my neck, in a flurry of wetness. I swallow hard. Not from fear like I would have three months ago, in anticipation. Mason is unpredictable.

"You've met Pricillia. This is Everett," he says, pointing to the brown-skinned woman, "and Cara." He points to the other woman.

"Please let's eat." He motions to the food.

Mason fills my goblet with champagne and the women pile my plates with fruit, cheese, crackers, and chicken, steak and potatoes—more food then I can eat in two meals.

"How are you doing, Sunshine?" Mason asks.

Everyone at the table stops moving as if the whole evening weighs on my answer.

"Well, thank you."

Mason smiles. "I trust you are being treated well here? No problems with any of the men?"

I shake my head. I take a draw of my champagne to wash down the bite of food I'd just taken. "Everyone has treated me just fine."

"If I opened the doors and said you could go home right now, would you leave me?"

I shift my eyes to his. How can he ask me that question? Does he want an honest answer? And if so, what could that cost me? I nod.

"Please answer with words, Sunshine. You are in a safe place. Would you leave me?"

I exhale the breath I was holding. "Yes, I would leave you."

His smile slips, and he deadpans. "Even after the kind treatment you have received here? You would leave me?" He puts his hands over his heart.

I sigh and choose my words carefully. "I appreciate your kindness; things could be so much worse for me." A dark wet cell comes to mind. "But, it's just that I had plans before I came here. I was supposed to be heading to school. I'm pretty sure I'd be engaged by now. So, I wouldn't leave as a slap in the face to you," I gesture toward him and offer a tight smile. "But to get my life back on track." I stare at him.

His lips pick up at the corners and a smile forms. "Well, this lifestyle isn't for everyone. I appreciate your honesty."

"Thank you." I relax a bit and resume my meal.

The other women resume chatting about this and that, along with Mason, as if we are not sitting naked at a table, preparing for lord knows what."

"Do you have a favorite lottery winner? By now, I'm sure you do. After three months, they should become more familiar."

I blush because I do. "Connell."

"Dammit." Mason slams the table, causing me to jump.

I slide my eyes to his with care. "Did I say something wrong?"

He laughs. "Nope. He bet me you'd say him." Mason gestures and Cara pops up. She has a perfect landing strip. She opens a door in the back of the room and Connell walks through, naked. His cock hanging heavy. I tear my eyes away from it and meet his eyes, finding him smiling.

"Have a seat." Mason points to the chair to my right.

Before Connell takes a seat, he kisses me on the mouth. "Thank you for having me, Mason."

Mason looks back and forth between the two of us with a smile, almost in a trance. His elbows propped up on the table, his hand under his chin. Connell takes my hand under the table.

"You seem happy," Connell says to Mason.

Mason claps his hands together. "Boy, do I have a surprise for the two of you. But later for that. Tonight, we eat and then we fuck."

This is insanity. I am sitting at a table with five naked people, eating fucking dinner as if nothing is odd about this. But I comply. I drink champagne and sample rich desserts and succulent meats and vegetables, exchanging pleasantries until my body is used for pleasure. I suppose all our bodies will be used for that purpose, but I'm almost certain I'm the only one who didn't choose to be here. Though I'm not sure about the three women. Are they willing employees like the groomers and the guard? Or, are they prisoners awaiting the end of their sentences like me?

"Time for dessert," Mason announces.

Everett stands and moves toward the head of the table. "Sunshine, this way please," she says.

On shaky legs, I rise. I have an idea about the rules of this world Mason has created. So far, he hasn't deviated from them. I am alive and unharmed if I don't count the psychological and emotional scars I will have forever. As long as I play along, I will remain alive and safe.

I climb the short steps leading to the table top and lie on my back on the navy cushion as directed. My legs are elevated and supported with padding that now extends from the table. Leave it to Mason to create a table this out of the ordinary. Nothing in this place is ordinary.

"Help yourselves," Mason says. Music begins playing, the lights dim, and only incandescent lighting remains. The song is dark and slow. The table shrinks in size as the sides fold down, leaving me on a narrower strip. The five of them stand around me, their faces are aglow with light. Even I have to admit how beautiful they all look. I steady myself for what is to come.

Mouths everywhere. Cara and Everett's mouths latch onto my nipples. I gasp as they lick and caress. My pussy already wet and ready, tightens in anticipation. I have never been with a woman before and from the way this is going, I will be with three.

Connell smiles at me before leaning forward and stroking my clit with his tongue. When I feel the weight and heaviness of Mason's cock, I am overcome. So many sensations at once. The pounding of his cock deep inside of me, my pussy contracting around it, Connell, licking and sucking my clit, while my nipples take a glorious beating. I am so close to coming that I don't hesitate to dine on the pussy that is hovering above me. Pricilla. She is straddling me. I spread her labia and wrap my lips around her clit, trying to copy Connell's approach. I lick and suck her clit, then drag my tongue over her opening. She throws her head back in pleasure, and I come apart. My mouth sucks harder and harder as I thrust my hips forward for more of Mason's cock until I can't move.

Mason trades places with Connell who slides inside of me and doesn't take long before he is coming deep inside of me.

6

NIKO

*I*n all my years on this planet I don't think I would have ever expected some shit like this to go down. I watch Whitney walk down the hallway.

I'm not a sentimental guy, but even *my* heart aches as I take in her broken form—head down, turtle-like cadence. Heartbroken. All I can think about is the piece of shit downstairs that she is returning to. She must either really love him or be one of the most scared and broken women on the planet. But I saw it, for the briefest second— hope filled her eyes when I agreed to her plan. Like I restored her faith in humanity. But I know the second she heads down that elevator Thomas the douchebag will shatter it again.

I would have never slept with her. Arrested her, yes. The second the money exchanged hands, I would have slapped the cuffs on her.

But now, I need to save her.

Thomas Ackerly is the lowest piece of shit on earth. He is the worst type of scum. I've been working this case for about seven months. When I met Thomas through mutual acquaintances it was easy to insert myself into this quaint beach town, and working at Milo's Gym as a trainer was the perfect cover.

The international crime task force that—my employer—was developed for just this type of criminal. My home base is in London. There I am known as an officer of the law. But, when I'm sent out on jobs, I'm the new guy—the new member of the community. I have traveled all over Europe, the US, and Australia. My newest assignment has landed me on the beautiful island of Barbados.

My specialty is little fish—catching them before they grow into sharks. Let the FBI, DEA, HLS, and the CIA go after the long-time criminal organizations. My goal is to get 'em before they ever have a chance.

Thomas Ackerly came up on my radar after he lost his money in the stock market and some desperation gambling. Lots of men lose everything to a bad decision—a risk they didn't think through. But a normal man would take the gut punch and rebuild, legally. Thomas has proven not to be a normal guy. He believes the world owes him his success, and he is willing to do anything to get it. The red flags went up when his name surfaced in some seriously sleazy underground gambling—dog fights, a short stint selling dope, sleazy bum fights, and a couple of prostitution near arrests.

Oh, that's the other thing—this island is small, and pretty boy Thomas is thought of as a prince among men. Meaning, when the police, his family, and society witnessed what could only be descried as his downward spiral they looked the other way. Brushed it off as growing pains.

It wasn't difficult to catch his attention. He's a desperate man.

I inserted myself into Thomas' life at Milo's, a local boxing gym. I got a job there as a trainer, and I offer personal security if anyone should need it.

It didn't take long. Me being the new guy to the island. I'm a white guy, a stand out on this island where almost everyone is some shade of brown. Within a month, Thomas was saddling up to me to become my friend. He used his manipulation skills to get free training sessions out of me, under the guise of a new brotherhood. He frequently presented me with business opportunities that were, what he referred to as, *hot* and needed me to move on them right away. His desperation and temper always brewed just below the surface—a pot of water waiting to boil over.

I was surprised when he came to me with this new venture. He wants to be a pimp. His ass will be in jail in no time, where men like him belong—off the streets.

The plan was simple. His prostitute would saunter into my room; I would make her feel welcome, flirt with her, promise her a good time, and then arrest her ass on the spot. Then, with the biggest smile on my face, I'd walk down to the restaurant and wipe the stupid smile Thomas has been wearing from his face when I arrest his ass too. After, I'd hop on the next plane back to London—I'm due for a vacation. I don't understand what all the fuss is over the sun. I am ready for some overcast days. Here, I feel like I'm in a perpetual half-eye squint.

Instead, I am sitting in the suite, stunned. My plans changed the second Whitney walked through the door. One look at her told me that she was not a pro. Then I learned just how evil Thomas really is. A man that can do this to a woman he is supposed to love is only getting started. The most vile and evil criminals started out less sick than Thomas. He has the potential to become a monster.

7

WHITNEY

I stop at the bar and order a drink before I face him. While the bartender goes to work, I shoot a text to my dad to come and get me. I text that Thomas has been drinking, and I'm tired and don't want him to drive me home. What I don't say is that Thomas is worse than the monster that took me. I don't have to wait long for Daddy's response. He would never leave me in a position to ride in the car with someone who's been drinking, and he certainly wouldn't want me to pay for a ride if he were available.

The bartender sets a shot in front of me and I down it and ask for a second shot.

Then I turn and watch Thomas. He looks happy.

He looks like a man who just received the best news on the planet. If he was visibly hurting over the fate he decided for me, I may be more forgiving. If his head was on the table, or if he was pacing back and forth staring repeatedly at his watch I may be able to see his point of view. But not Thomas, he is already enjoying all the riches he expects from me being on my back.

If only he knew his new business venture stalled out before it could even get off the ground. I down the second shot, place cash on the bar and take brave steps toward what used to be my future—toward the man I believed in and gave me something to hope for when I was in The Chamber.

It seems like forever before I reach his table. He doesn't even bother to look up at me when I take my seat. He doesn't smile, and he barely acknowledges me. "How'd it go?" he asks without looking up. His jaw clenching is the only reaction giving away how he might be feeling. *Is he upset with me?*

"It's done," I say under my breath.

"Good. You hungry?"

I shake my head. He takes the ring box and holds it up. "We'll talk about this later." He pockets the ring.

After what he thinks I've done for him, he is holding the engagement over my head? This is worse than I thought. Nikolai is right, I need to get away from him.

"I promise next time will be easier," he says and plants a chaste kiss on my cheek. He stares out at nothing, still not looking directly at me. The look is a mixture of disgust and pride. The fact that he is directing his eyes everywhere but toward me fills me with hurt. "He pay you?"

I nod.

"You still in the mood?" he asks, smiling and glancing at me for the first time.

The look makes my stomach knot.

Are you insane? "No."

He smirks. "Figures. You can slip me my money when we get into the car."

His money. It hasn't even been a day of our supposed business venture and it's already his money? He is exactly what Nikolai said he was, a dangerous and desperate man.

Thomas wipes his mouth and pats his stomach. His eyes find mine again. "You sure you don't want to go upstairs for the night, we have the suite until morning?" he asks and reaches for my hand. I snatch my hand away before he can touch me.

He looks at me like he's seeing me for the first time. His face registers shock before he can cover it when he takes in my tear-stricken face. This time, he takes my hand and doesn't give me the chance to snatch it away. His fingers are a vice around mine, making me wince.

"Listen, I need this and you need me. So, I'd appreciate it if you don't try to make me look like the bad guy or feel like shit when you've been screwing strangers for a fucking year," he says, through clenched teeth before he releases my hand. I immediately nurse the sting, rubbing the top of my hand tenderly.

"I'm tired, Thomas. I'm ready to go home."

"But, I'm not. We aren't wasting that suite upstairs. The customer shouldn't be the only one tasting the nectar. You haven't shared since you returned," he slurs the words, his islander accent more pronounced.

Sirens blare inside my head, sounding more like a scream. On the inside, I am breaking in two. I inhale a healthy dose of air before I speak again. I take in my surroundings. There are a lot of people around us. Surely, I'm safe. The thought hurts more than I expected.

"Look, a lot has happened. You've been drinking, I've been drinking. My dad is on his way."

Thomas looks at me as if I've lost my mind. He gets close to my face causing me to jump. He must smell the fear emitting from my body.

"You are mine. I can take care of you. I will see you home when we're done." His expression softens toward me. "Call him and tell him I will bring you home when I'm ready."

"It's fine, Daddy is probably out front, and he'd be upset if he drove all the way here."

Thomas takes a moment, and when he looks up at me it's with concern, his mood changing drastically. "We're gonna be okay. This won't last forever, and I appreciate you representing our team like a queen." He runs the back of his hand down the side of my cheek, causing my blood to ice.

Oh, he is good. First, he acts like he loves me, then he hates me, and now he loves me again. I pull the envelope out of my purse, stand up, and push it across the small table to him.

"Enjoy the suite and fuck off." I walk away. My body shakes with nerves and fear.

I should have known that he wouldn't give up so easy. Thomas doesn't want to make a scene, so he matches my pace until we exit the crowded restaurant.

Once we are in the empty hall leading to the lobby, he grabs me by the arm and spins me around to face him. His eyes are crazed. I don't know if I'm witnessing drunken behavior or subdued rage because Thomas has never shown me either.

"This. Isn't. Over. You and I started something tonight. While you were upstairs fucking another stranger, I was downstairs working. I have clients lined up for the next two weeks." He flashes two fingers in front of my face and doesn't care that I flinch.

He doesn't care about how distraught I am.

He believes that I went upstairs and screwed a stranger like it was another day at the office. "Let me go," I say through gritted teeth. "Now, or I scream."

"You wouldn't."

I take a deep breath preparing my lungs when he lets go. I can't get away from him fast enough. I resist every urge to run. My face is wet with tears, and the sobs tear through me painfully as I make my way to the downstairs lobby.

8

WHITNEY

*T*hankfully, Daddy doesn't ask me any questions on the car ride home. Instead, he rubs my arm with his free hand and lets me cry silent tears until my well runs dry. My body is heavy when I pour myself from the car. I am almost to my room when my dad speaks up. "If you need to talk, I'm here for you."

I turn and look at him, his face mirrors my pain. I hate that my family is suffering because of me. "Did he hurt you?" he asks.

I nod before speaking. What I want to say is, he is a horrible human being that wants me to do horrendous things. What I actually say is, "Thomas is fine; it's not him, it's me. He proposed, sort of. But then things got all weird." I wring my hands and the lie continues to formulate in my mind. "I guess I'm not ready for future talk. I need to focus on getting over the last year, and he wants to act like it never happened."

My dad takes the few steps to me. "Baby girl, you take all the time you need. I think we all want to pretend that the last year was just a nightmare and didn't really happen. Knowing how much you suffered is a struggle for all of us—I felt helpless every second you were gone."

A shiver runs through me. "I know, Daddy."

He wraps his arms around me. "We'll get through this."

I nod again. "Thanks, Daddy," I say and squeeze him. "I love you."

"Love you, too."

He waits for me to walk into my room, and when I turn to close my door I glance at my dad and see a forced smile on his face and worry marking his eyes.

There is nothing I can do to make sense of what happened tonight. I lied to my father when I shouldn't have. Somehow, I couldn't bare the worry and pity that would come with me telling him the truth. I can't stand everyone looking at me this way. Plus, Daddy would try to kill Thomas, and while I might enjoy that after tonight, I can't help but think Thomas is only behaving this way out of desperation.

There is no way I can see Thomas again. He would rather manipulate and take advantage of me than love me through the trauma of last year.

I lie back on my bed and think back to that fateful day that ruined everything.

∿

I PARKED MY BMW 18—A graduation present from my grandparents—in the parking garage at The Beachcomber shopping center on the same level as the main entrance so I wouldn't have to take the stairs or the elevator. I should have checked with the girls and parked on the same level as they did, but it was daytime, and I thought, what could really happen to you in the middle of the day? Boy was I stupid to think that.

I spotted my friends easily—Chalice with her long, dark hair and light brown skin, not quite as light as mine, but most people ask if we are sisters. We are both a mix of mostly African, but also some Irish and Native American; we swore we'd do our genealogy charts but never actually went through with it. Amaris looks exotic, with her deep ebony skin that never has a blemish; she's simply gorgeous. She never intended on modeling, but by the age thirteen, she was already signed with a major agency.

The three of us have been friends since we were five years old. All different, yet all supportive of each other's paths. Amaris was homeschooled and tutored, and Chalice followed the normal path, graduating from a public school on-time. No amount of time or distance would split up our squad.

"Ladies!" I shouted out when I made it to our usual spot, the food court entrance.

"Whit!" they both rang out in unison. We ran into each other's arms as if we haven't seen one another in weeks, when in reality we had seen each other two days ago.

"Are ya ready to shop till we drop?" Amaris asked, her islander accent changed by her travels to new and far off places.

"Absolutely!" My face splits with excitement.

"Bring it on!" Chalice added.

We all cracked up and walked arm and arm—three gorgeous, young black women who were each other's favorite people in the entire world.

After hours of shopping, we fell into our seats at the restaurant, exhausted but successful. Chalice found a tastefully slinky lavender dress, Amaris' canary strapless dress made her skin look sinful, and I believed I just may stop Thomas' heart when he sees me in my fitted, short red dress.

"Waters all around, please," I asked the server.

Chalice clears her throat. "We did it, ladies! Our guys are going to lose it when they see us tonight."

"What guy?" Amaris asked.

We both reach out to her in consolation. "I forgot; sorry, sweets," Chalice apologized.

"I'm fine. I didn't really expect Fredrick to be able to handle me being gone so much anyway. Besides, there's this new guy that I really like," Amaris admitted.

"We're listening," Chalice exclaimed as we both offered our full attention.

"Let's just say three little letters, N-B and A." Amaris awaited our reactions.

We both gasped. Amaris is tall, like five-ten, and she has always complained about how hard it was to meet a tall guy. "You found Mr. Tall guy! Finally!" I teased.

"We met a couple of weeks ago while I was in LA. He is very sweet. We've been chatting back and forth."

"Too bad he isn't a footballer . You know I am much more of a football fan," Chalice loves football.

We all laughed. Leave it to Chalice to think of herself.

"Hey, Whit, do you think Thomas will pop the question at the garden party tonight?" Chalice asked.

I shook my head at my crazy friend. "How would I know? Just because you saw him leaving a jewelry store doesn't mean he was ring shopping."

"It's been two years, sweets! And you are leaving for London. A gorgeous lass like you with all those brains up in your head, he'd be a fool not to snatch you up. I bet he makes it official at the party," Chalice offered.

I turned to Amaris. "And what say you, my dear friend?"

Amaris' wicked smile grows. She rubs her hands together as if she is going to reveal a master plan. "It goes something like this. A handsome fellow, a gorgeous lady, a beautiful locale, an important question, an affirmative answer, and you know the rest."

I could only dare hope that was true, because Thomas was it for me, my sun and moon. I would have to control myself so I didn't blurt out yes before he completed his proposal. It would have been so wonderful with my family and all our Province's families there.

"All right, ladies, it's time for us to get home and get ready!" I squealed.

"So true," Chalice said. "Time for me to get home and cock-up."

I shook my head at her. "Just say take a nap."

"Where did you park, lass?" Amaris asked me.

"On the first level; how about you guys?"

"We rode together. You want an escort to your car?"

"Me? Of course not. It's broad daylight, what could happen?"

My gals shook their heads at me. We hugged and headed to our cars.

I didn't make it to my car. Three men walked towards the mall entrance—shoppers like me. I made eye contact like my daddy always said I should to show confidence and not fear. We barely passed each other before they were on me. No more island party, no more possible engagement, no more me.

When I came to I was afraid to open my eyes. I knew I was on an airplane, I felt the push and pull of the engine—the subtle weightlessness. I kept my eyes closed for fear of what I would find when I opened them. No amount of curiosity could've forced my eyes open.

Instead I listened. For anything that may have helped me, though I knew nothing would. Terrible thoughts ran through my head. I will never see my parents again. I will never see Chalice and Amaris again, and my Thomas. What will come of him? He was perfect for me. What sick person takes a woman from her life? You can't just steal a person. Deep voices broke my train of thought.

"This year's selection is the best one so far," a heavy voice called out.

"Bet. Too bad your ass drew the short straw on getting Chamber guard duty this year. I hope I get assigned to this piece right here. I will blow her back out every chance I get," the second voice said.

My heart beat sped up and I had to control my breathing. The cabin of the aircraft was very quiet. One gasp and they would've know I was awake.

"Don't brag, Money, you know Dominic is gonna be watching you like a hawk, always does," deep voice said.

"You didn't hear?" Money said.

"Here what?"

"Seems Dominic decided to join us in the rotation this year. I guess one of these sizzling pieces got his attention. He's guarding this year," Money said.

"What?" his deep voice sounded excited.

I stopped listening to the goons who nabbed me because all of their sex talk made my knees weak. Welcomed sleep found me, and I dreamt.

I dreamt of beautiful elegant dresses and garden parties.

I dreamt of delicious food and drink.

And I dreamt of my Thomas proposing marriage.

In an instant, my beautiful dreams turned into a nightmare. I was chained to a concrete wall, given enough food to sustain life. My body used for the amusement of others, beaten regularly for resisting and daring to fight back. I awoke to my screams.

"There, there, my dear. It was only a nightmare," Money said.

The one speaking to me, Money, moved toward me. He was larger than his voice would suggest. Caucasian, tall and very well built—strong. Eyes pale blue and light brown hair. He was very attractive, but his actions toward me made him ugly.

I couldn't pretend to sleep any longer, so I followed what my father said and made eye-contact, even though everything in my soul said to close my eyes. "It would seem that I have awoken from one nightmare to find myself in the middle of another," I said.

He took a seat across from mine. "Now, now. The Chamber isn't as bad as you might think. My name is Montreal, but everybody calls me Money." He snickered and oriented his head toward the monstrosity behind him. "The big guy is Luther."

I turned my head to find the guy he referred to as Luther. He looked like a Luther. Dark brown skin, shaved head, and muscles on top of his muscles. I swallowed the lump in my throat. I never stood a chance.

I SHAKE the memory from my mind. Nauseous and dizzy, part of my brain can't believe that I suffered The Chamber, and better yet, survived it.

It doesn't take long before the stress of the night settles into my body and sleep takes me. I am thankful for heavy, dark sleep, with no dreams.

When I awaken, I feel the effects of the alcohol I drank last night. I rarely drink, a cocktail here or there is more my speed, but last night required so much more. I have no idea what I'm going to do. Part of me is hoping Thomas takes the hint from last night and doesn't darken my doorstep, and part of me hopes he does. *Could I forgive him? If he asked me?* At least he accepts me for what happened in some capacity, which might be the most I can ask of anyone.

9

WHITNEY

*T*oday is my therapy appointment. I breeze through breakfast and hop into the car with my dad. He hasn't let me drive anywhere without someone since I've been home. I don't fight his need to protect me; I'd be the same way with my own child.

"I'll be right here in an hour," he reassures me.

"Thanks, Daddy," I say and kiss his cheek. The sky is a soft powdery blue without a single cloud. I prefer the clouds; they give the sky something extra. Dr. Wesley's office boasts enormous windows that face the ocean. It's a perfect view for me and my nerves.

I walk into the office and take a seat in the small waiting room. The receptionist smiles at me. "Good morning, Whitney."

I return her smile. "Good morning, Lucy."

The wait only takes about ten minutes before Lucy is sending me into the office. As always, I am greeted with warmth the second I cross the threshold. The floor is carpeted with thick, cushiony earth tones. The furniture is dark brown and black. There is a fire place and mantle, green plants in every corner, and tranquil art on the wall that allows us patients a moment's escape when the session gets tough. Dr. Wesley did a good job of making her office look more like a family room, rather than an office. I was nervous about my parents' choice for my therapist. I've known Dr. Wesley, Maxine, my whole life. She was close friends with my oldest sister, Joey, growing up, and Thomas' cousin. But, she is the best therapist on the island. Daddy also made the point that if I wanted a therapist not known to us in any capacity, we'd have to travel. Our community is a close knit one. So, I decided to give it a try, and actually, she and I knowing each other hasn't been an issue so far. She and I have been meeting twice a week since my return, and I'm not sure if it's helping yet.

"Good morning, Whitney."

"Morning," I say and take my seat across from her, nearest to the windows. Her smile is warm and comforting. I've known her to be quite chatty, but in here she isn't a conversationalist. I mean, I guess I'm supposed to do all the talking—well most of it.

"How have you been since the last time we met?"

I shrug. "Okay, I guess."

"Any new dreams?"

"Last night. But it wasn't a dream. It was a memory, a bad one."

"I'm listening."

I take a deep breath and turn to the window and allow myself to get lost in the ocean before returning to her. "It was the one from the day I was taken, but more details. It was so real, like I was there."

She leans forward. "*Because you were.*" She pauses to give me time to process what she said. "Our memories happened to us, Whitney. The more significant the event you are remembering, the more intense the memory will be. Emotions are not always tied to our dreams, but our memories are intertwined with them." She leans back. "Did you change anything this time?"

She asks this because sometimes I imagine the events differently so I don't get taken, choosing a different path—ride with my gals, get a ride, park on the same level as them. Instead of taking a break from school, I accept my admission to University College the first time. "No, this time I end up on the plane. I end up at The Chamber."

"I see." She writes on her tablet.

"Why do I always think of that day? I feel stuck in that moment."

"You have to give yourself time to adjust and adapt. PTSD can be debilitating, but the more you understand about that stuck feeling, the better equipped you will be at dealing with it. That place of being stuck in '*what if*' comes from feeling responsible for what happened to you. It stems from a belief that somehow this was your fault. It's normal. You ask yourself, what if I went a different way, or stayed home. I counter with what if you did decide to ride with your friends. You said there were three men?"

I nod.

"They could have easily taken all three of you."

I shiver at the thought.

"It's scary to think about all of the things that are out of our control, but Whitney, you are here, which is already a step in the right direction. You are going to re-experience the trauma in dreams; a smell could be a trigger. And, when this happens it makes you feel out of control in that moment, right?"

Tears well in my eyes. "Yes. It's paralyzing."

She hands me a tissue. "Do you understand why?"

I shake my head. "I mean, I think because it feels so real."

"Yes. That is a big part of it. Also, when you re-experience the trauma your instincts take over. *You* are no longer in control—these are survival instincts and when they take control, your stressors kick into

life or death mode—also called flight or fight. That's why we have to
create opportunities for you to talk openly and remember the details
of the trauma in a controlled and safe environment, like this office.
The more you experience the traumatic event, the less likely it is for
the emotions and memories surrounding the event will catch you by
surprise. It will become a part of your life, like any memory—but
with the right set of tools you can react to it more like recalling an
unwanted memory from your past, like for example the death of a
loved one, and less like a murderer stalking toward you. It's called
Prolonged Exposure Therapy."

She sits back in her seat and gives me a second to process. I do so,
staring out at the vast ocean; secretly I wish it would devour me. I
would never tell her that.

"When you were here last, we were beginning to discuss what
happened once the plane landed." She flips through pages on her
tablet; she's old school. "Take me back there, please."

The look I give her asks, *do I have to?* Her response is a nod. She and I
both know I have to, but I don't want to. I take a few deep breaths.

"The two big men. Luther and Montreal take me off the plane. They
put a hood over my head before they open the door. I can't see
anything, but I know I'm getting into a car. My face is drenched
because my hands are bound, and I am crying. I try hard to clear my
mind of the fear but I can't. I think about not seeing my family and
friends ever again. I think about Thomas, too."

Dr. Wesley doesn't interrupt me. Up to today, we hadn't ventured past
my actual abduction, mostly because I couldn't get past why it
happened to me. She convinced me that I'm not special. Not in a
mean way, but in a way to say God didn't choose this for me. She
made me understand that I was victim to a crazy person who has his
own freewill. She reminded me of the harsh reality that people are
kidnapped or worse every single day. This didn't make me feel better,

but knowing that I'm not alone helped somehow. Then she signed me up for a trauma group.

"The car stops and they take me out of it. It's breezy outside, but I'm not outside long before I'm inside again. It's dark. One of the men helps me up a winding staircase." My body chills with the memory so real that I'm freezing. "I'm pushed onto my knees, not hard, maybe guided is a better word. The hood is taken from my head. I don't open my eyes for a long time. I'm too scared. I don't want to see my new reality. I sob as silently as I can. Then my arms are set free. I only open my eyes when I hear other louder sobs. I'm not the only girl."

I pause to take a deep breath. I hadn't realized my eyes were closed, and when I open them light floods my vision. Dr. Wesley is a patient woman.

"I take in everything all at once. The room looks ancient. With a high ceiling and walls of stone. I count six other women in line with me— all frightened, all crying. I want to look behind me, but I don't. Instead, I stay as still as I can and I pray silently and say goodbye to everyone I love. That's when he rises from an opening in the floor that wasn't there before, in a flood of light. Oozing and dripping narcissism, egocentrism, charming, and smooth, the devil himself appears."

"Who are you speaking of?"

I shudder at the vision— the moment I came face-to-face with my captor. I fight the sobs, but they tear through me against my will. In my memory, he is shrouded with so much light it's blinding.

"Mason."

I jump up from my seat, my body shaking. Dr. Wesley sits silently as I pace the room. It seems like forever before I calm myself. I take a different seat in her office, as if this will help me.

"*You are safe, Whitney.* Say that aloud."

It takes a minute before I can because I have the hiccups now. "I am safe."

"I want you to walk over to the window and look out. See where you are."

I do as I'm told and stare out the window. "I'm home," I say and let the warmth of the sun wash over me, even if I can't actually feel it.

The timer buzzes and I send thank yous up to the heavens. There was no way I could delve further without suffering a nightmare later.

"How do you feel?"

"Tired." No one tells you the struggle and journey that happens after. I prayed for release, to be returned home safe, and here I am. The sad scary fact is I don't know when and if I will ever truly be free of that place. I omit many things from my therapy sessions. The things that leave me heavy with exhaustion, guilt. Why did I stay? When I was given the chance to leave, why didn't I take it. Connell? I don't think I can ever admit the feelings that I had for him. I'll never know if it was love. I know I will probably never see him again, but he will always have a secret special place in my heart. I exhale.

"I am going to give you a prescription for sleeping pills. I don't want you to take them every day, but definitely on the days that we meet. The therapeutic process can be brutal, and we heal during sleep," she says as she scribbles on a prescription pad. She hands me the paper and I take it.

"Thank you."

"You are much stronger than you know. Remember what you survived. You are a fighter; even if you don't believe that yet, you will." She gives me a hug. She always ends our session with a big hug. I welcome the contact; the pressure calms me.

10

WHITNEY

I wave goodbye to the receptionist and head for the door. This was a good session. I'm tired but not as exhausted as I usually feel. I round the corner to the lobby expecting to see Daddy, but Thomas stands in his place. My heart stutters. *What is he doing here?* The last time I saw him I told him to fuck off. But here he stands.

"What are you doing here, Thomas?" Fear courses through me, and my feet stick to the ground when they should move, fast.

He walks up to me and wraps me in his arms. I don't find the same comfort. "I missed you, and I owe you a lot of apologies and explanations for last night."

I don't acknowledge his words. "Did my father call you? How did you know I was here?"

"Yes. I called him, told him about our rough night and how miserable I was for rushing you. He was pleased and told me where you were so I could surprise you." He flashes his stunning smile. His handsomeness is so confusing. Is he the devil in another form or is he my Thomas, lost and in need of as much help as me?

"You told him what you asked of me?"

His face registers shock. "Of course not. I omitted certain details from the story. Come on, Whit, we belong together. Your family knows it, your friends know it. I know it, and so do you. Let's go grab lunch." He flashes that grin again.

This time, Thomas doesn't try so hard with a fancy meal. He pulls into a drive-thru fast food place that brings the food to the car while your car faces the ocean. *Nice choice.* I close my eyes while he orders. I listen to waves crashing onto the beach and inhale the salty air. With each exhalation I feel more at ease.

The car is thick with silence and a palpable energy that I can't read. The ball is in his court, and I'm sure he knows it.

"I'm sorry, eh," he finally says between bites of food. We are facing forward using our meal of cheeseburgers and fries as an escape, something to focus on. "I should have never pushed you or sprung that shit on you. I should have talked to you first. I guess I got lost in dollar signs."

A smirk forms on my face accompanied by a sound that travels from deep inside my throat. "Why was it okay for you to expect that from me to begin with? You want your girlfriend to sleep with other men, for money?" This time I turn to him and wait for his answer.

He stops eating. "I thought since you had experience doing it already, it wouldn't be too much to ask. I wanted someone I could trust."

"I was kidnapped. Flown across a great distance, and I was locked away with armed guards in a castle for a year. The only time I saw the sky was through a skylight I couldn't reach with a twenty-foot pole. Just because I didn't escape, doesn't mean I wanted to be there. I told you, Thomas, the guy had pictures of my family, my friends, you, from two years before he took me. He threatened everyone I loved. But make no mistake, Thomas, I hated every second of my life there."

He returns his attention to his burger. "It's about the sacrifice. We do this, and we go into our future together never wanting for anything."

What? "You still want me to do this? I thought you were apologizing to me because you changed your mind." It takes everything inside of me not to cry. These aren't tears of sadness; I'm pissed. I would never have gone with him if I knew he still wanted this for me.

He turns and looks at me. His face isn't angry or sad. He has hope in his eyes. "Yes. I still want this. We've already begun. I wanted to apologize for rushing you, for assuming you'd be ready to go full throttle, and for being a dick and holding *this* over your head." He pulls the ring out. "Whitney, I love you. You are a boss and a superwoman. We can do this together, make a fortune and stop. Go anywhere you want. Do anything you want." He slides the ring onto my finger. "Can you make this sacrifice for us if I promise we'll start slow?"

I gaze down at the beautiful diamond. A symbol that promises so much. "And what sacrifices are you making, Thomas?"

I can tell my question infuriates him. He has shown me in the last couple of days that a temper simmers beneath his smooth façade. "Why do you think I was drinking so much while you were upstairs last night?"

I shrug my shoulders. "You were celebrating."

He shakes his head and turns his gaze to mine. "It took everything in the very deepest parts of me not to run up those stairs and get you, to stop you. Every minute you were gone was killing me, knowing what you were sacrificing for us. I hated myself for what I'd asked, but I stayed in my seat because I can see what's on the other side. The bountiful life this gets us. We are a team, and I love you so much." He leans forward and places a gentle kiss onto my lips.

He makes my head hurt with the confusion he is causing me. "Can I think about it?" I ask.

He takes a moment before saying, "Sure, babe. You wanna go walk off these burgers?"

I shake my head. "I need to get home and take a nap. My therapy sessions are exhausting."

Thomas starts the car. "Are they helping you?"

I shrug again. "So far, I can't say. But it's only been a few weeks. I'll see with more time. I mean, I always feel better when I'm there but then when I leave, the world and reality hit me—I don't know how I feel."

Thomas grabs our trash and tosses it in the large can outside of his driver's side window, then backs out of the space. "Therapy is a waste of money. I'm all the therapy you need. If you want to talk, I'm all ears. I want to be here for you."

He looks at me and I can feel love pouring from his eyes. Maybe I was wrong about him. Maybe he's an opportunist who really believes this will be easy for me. In a way, he is right. By the time I was halfway through my year at The Chamber, I had adapted to my life there, we all had. It had become just sex. We were treated well, had everything we needed and more. The best of everything was afforded to us. Mason was a true evil genius. The seven of us formed an unshakeable bond, stronger together. The worst that ever happened to us had been the nights we had to have sex, but we were even given days off. If what Thomas was proposing was anything like that, perhaps I could adapt to that, too. Anything was better than him leaving me. The thought of being alone is worse than anything I'd suffered. Besides, who else would want me after knowing about The Chamber?

We pull up in front of my house and Thomas parks. "Tell me you'll think about it."

I offer him a smile. Maybe this could work. "I will."

Thomas leans towards me and kisses me. This time it isn't chaste or sweet. It's heavy with want. His lips taste mine, and his tongue sweeps across them requesting entrance. I break the kiss before granting permission. My head is light. Him wanting me after all of this is a welcomed surprise, though I don't know how ready I am for that.

11

"Welcome," Connell's voice says. I can't see him, but after spending so much time with him, I know his voice well. In recent months, every action he has toward me has been confusing. Unnatural for this space we exist in. He smiles so much around me, staring as if he is seeing through me. Choosing to spend some nights talking over a simple dinner.

I asked the other girls how he interacts with them, and they've said he is polite but all about business. Recently, they've been mentioning that he hasn't been visiting them at all, and they were surprised when I reported that he hadn't missed meeting with me once.

The blindfold is removed from my eyes. It takes a second to adjust to my surroundings. One thing I know for sure, I am no longer inside the walls of The Chamber. The space is massive, a cabin from the large planks of wood that seem to encapsulate the structure. There is a back wall of windows that only show darkness.

"Where are we?" I ask him as my throat tightens and my internal alarms blare.

"Anywhere."

I sigh and shrug. "Am I going to get in trouble for being here?"

Connell steps closer to me, removing my heavy coat. He stands behind me, kissing my bare shoulders. I am only wearing a sheer yellow silky nightgown and silver stilettos, my hair in natural curls down my back. My eyes say what my words can't as tremors take hold. Have I been kidnapped again, this time by Connell? He waits for my reaction, but I only stare at him and wait for him to explain why I am no longer inside the walls of The Chamber.

Montreal steps forward with another guard I recognize. I take a couple of quick deep breaths, my head is light and swirly. But, if my guard is here, then Mason must know I am here. I give nothing away, yet. I have the right to wait and have my question answered. I might not have much control over my life, but it is still mine.

Montreal opens a tablet and Mason's image appears on the screen.

"Sunshine." He waves to me, and I meet his gesture with a tight smile. "Enjoy a couple of nights away from the madness of The Chamber. This was a highly unusual request from one of my lottery winners. However, for the right price, I'm all for trying new things." His smile is grand and meets his eyes before he falls dead serious. "I trust you to be on your best behavior."

I nod. "Yes."

"Montreal and Wilbert will be downstairs if you should need assistance."

"Thank you," I say.

Mason's face is gone. Montreal and Wilbert rush off, and I am alone with Connell.

He takes me by the hand and leads me to a sofa. I take his lead and sit.

"Are you okay with this?" His expression is unsure. "If not, I can have the guards take you back." He appears younger on the outside as if I am seeing him in real life for the first time. Some of his usual smooth confidence has faded. He and I have an undeniable connection. I'm not the only girl to experience something extra here. Flame seems to have Dominic wrapped around her finger. Sapphire most assuredly is falling in love with Mason. Even sweet, shy Sky has an LW who has expressed an interest in her. In this most strange and sad place, human relationships have formed. The more human men have developed concern and protective instincts for us. In return, we have extended a Stockholm-like olive branch, if in the beginning only for sanity's sake.

I pat his leg. "This is amazing." When I inhale, the air is rich with cedar and clean scent of lemon and lavender. I close my eyes and let the deep breaths relax me at the realization that I am not inside the dreaded Chamber walls, if only for a short time.

He hands me a glass of wine, an action that he has done many times. I take a sip, and it is sweet and refreshing. Connell picks up a remote, depresses a button and the back window slides open. The air is brisk but welcome. By my count, it's November. He presses another button, and the area lights up, warm, incandescent lights glow, and I see a small table with two chairs and candles in the center.

"May I?" I ask.

He stands and reaches out for my hand. I hesitate and stare at his hand, before taking it. What does all of this mean? I slide my eyes up to meet his, and they are welcome and warm, as if he is saying *this is a safe space, you can trust me.*

I take his hand and follow him toward the opening. The balcony, like everything else I've seen, is thick with heavy logs. The sky is bright with stars, the heavy packed white powder is everywhere. A cold shiver runs through my body.

"Just one second." He disappears and returns with a heavy blanket and wraps it around my shoulders.

"Thank you."

He disappears again, and I take a seat at the table. I stare out at the darkness and relax as cool air bathes me. Other than the unreachable skylights that recess and open in The Chamber, I haven't been outside in seven months. The moon is big and bright and mysterious. I wonder what Thomas is doing right now. It's been so long, he has to have moved on by now. Why would he wait for me? It's not like Mason sent letters to our families promising our release. My family must be going crazy, numbed somehow by time and the unknown. Worry still there, but shelved in a special place to continue living.

He returns with a steaming cup of coffee. I stare up at him. He really is a gorgeous man.

"This is so beautiful; the fresh air takes my breath away."

"Whitney, you take my breath away." He started calling me by my real name a few months ago. I should have stopped him, hearing it felt so real. Sunshine is another side of me, Whitney is the real me, but I never corrected him. I asked him if I could know his real name and he told me I've always known it.

I smile at his sentiment.

"How did you arrange this?" I ask after I swallow my first sip of coffee, made with enough cream to give it a smooth, rich taste, and two sugars, just how I like it.

He reaches his hand across the table and takes my hands in his. "I paid Mason a lot of money to get you alone outside of those walls. I wanted to talk to you about something, away from that place."

He exhales and continues. "It seems I've had a change of heart. I was so excited about being selected to participate in the seventh group of lottery winners. I was willing to pay anything to be there. When I got the call, it really was like winning a lottery. Seven beautiful women, mine for the taking for an entire year."

I look away when he says the word "taking," because that is precisely what we are. Their's for the taking. Not asked, permission not granted. I try to pull my hands back, but he squeezes and holds on.

"But, this is wrong. My money has given me freedom and unlimited resources, but it is wrong for me to use it to buy people. Beautiful helpless victims. And we come in like knights in fucking shining armor like we are here to make all of your dreams come true." He stares down at our hands and spits the last words. "Who am I? What makes me so goddamned special that I get to take part in something like this? I'm sorry for everything that you have been put through."

Tears fall from my eyes. "You always seemed so happy to be there." I stare into his eyes.

His lips form a hard line, and he looks away. I don't. When he returns his eyes to mine his expression is laced with guilt. "At first I was happy. This was everything I thought I wanted. Then it wasn't."

He reaches across the small table and wipes my tears with his thumb and caresses my cheek.

"I am withdrawing from the group."

Panic shoots through me. Connell is the kindest person I have met there. The time we've spent together has changed so much over the months. What started out as rough and wild sex has turned into something deeper, a connection. "You're leaving?"

"It's not the same for me anymore. You see, I've fallen in love with one of the women."

"Who?" I ask, but I think I know the answer.

"You, Whitney."

I look down. I can't believe he's saying this to me.

He tugs at my chin so that I am looking directly at him. "I don't want to be with anybody else but you."

He is still holding one of my hands. "I don't expect you to respond to that. Our situations are different. I have choices, and you don't, but I'd like to give you one."

More tears spill because it doesn't take a genius to know what is coming next. "I'm listening."

He takes a couple of deep breaths and exhales. What I think is coming is something of grave importance to him. "Come with me. Tonight. I already have transportation ready to take you away from here."

I don't say anything. What can I say? Yes, I'll run away with you. He has told me how he feels about me but never asked me what I think about him.

I shake my head. I will miss his companionship, but how can I go without permission? My family could be harmed for my selfishness. I'm more than half-way through this shit. Leaving now would be like quitting a twenty-six-mile marathon at mile twenty. I've already come so far.

"You don't want to come with me." His shoulder's sag and the air of hope leaks out of him.

I squeeze his hands. "There is no way I can run away from this place, no matter how much I want to. I was chosen to complete a year sentence, and I am nearly done. It would be selfish to leave when my family could be punished for it."

I pull away from him and get up from the table. I stand at the balcony and stare out at the whiteness. So much white. Freedom is beyond this log castle. I feel warmth and pressure from his arms as they engulf me. I lean my head against his chest. "You don't love me yet. I don't expect you to in our situation, but you would if given a chance."

I turn in his arms and look up at him. "What about the man I have back home?"

Connell shakes his head, kisses me quick and chaste on the lips. The sensation coupled with cold air stirs something inside and my stomach clenches.

"He isn't enough for you."

I stare up into his eyes. "And you are?"

A sort of a small laugh escapes him. "I could be if you let me."

I rest my head on his muscular chest. "We'd always have the memory of this place, of what I did here and what you came here to do hanging over us."

He rests his chin on my head. "I'd spend a lifetime garnering your forgiveness and helping you heal from your wounds. Come with me, Whitney. I can keep you safe." It's a whisper, a heavy plea.

I don't answer him. What can I say? I can't go with him.

"When are you leaving?"

"Tonight."

My heart aches. Could I be feeling love in the tiny fissures tearing shards through me?

"I don't want you to go." I squeeze him.

He pulls away from me and takes me by the hand. I follow him up a wide and heavy staircase and into a massive bedroom. An oversized bed dressed in romantic white and gray bedding and fluffy pillows is welcoming. Not a stitch of yellow. In the center of the room a claw foot tub, and windows line the outside wall. Connell turns on the tub, and the force of the water suggests it will be full quickly.

He returns to me, wordless. He grabs one of the thin straps of my gown and looks into my eyes for permission. I give it to him. My chest rises with haste. We've done this before, but never outside. He is slow in pace as he pulls my right strap, then my left, and shimmies my gown down my body. My nipples tighten as the cold air hits them. He steps back and stares admiringly at me. I take deep breaths and wait. I watch him watch me.

The sound of rushing water clouds the space. He doesn't touch me. Only admires. His smile reaching his eyes. When we first met, I could tell for him it was all a big game. Sex and folly. I know he never meant for emotions to enter the playing field.

He turns and leaves me standing there.

I watch him as he bends over and turns off the water. Then strips out of his clothes. His body is taut. He steps into the tub. His smooth abdominal muscles contract into at least eight sections as he sucks in air and exhales it. His erection at attention, poised to strike like a snake. He reaches his hand out to me, and I close the short distance. I take his hand and allow him to help me step into the bath. He sits behind me, and I take the space between his legs.

He presses a couple buttons on a remote: one lights up the outdoor space beyond the windows, revealing snow covered trees and the full moon. The other filters soft music through the room.

The water settles just under our shoulders. His cock pressed against my back. I want to do things to it, to him.

He picks up a sponge, plunges it into the tub and squeezes it out on my exposed skin.

"Hmm." The warm water is divine.

He drops the sponge, and his hands wrap around me. I lay my head against his chest. "I wish I met you in any other circumstance. Connell, I know I could love you. I just don't know if I can now. I don't know how we could ever move forward from this, this place. I don't want you to leave me." There I say it. The words that popped into my head when he first told me his plan. "I don't know if I can finish out my time here without you." The last part comes out weak and shaky.

He kisses my neck and the space behind my ear. "I can't stay here knowing what is happening to you. While other men touch you. It's already slowly killing me." He continues peppering me with his lips, sucking in places, licking in others. Warm sensations cause me to clench my thighs.

I squeeze my eyes shut at his words. "Does Mason know you are leaving?"

He stops in the middle of a kiss on my shoulder. His lips press down. "Not yet. I don't think he would of let me bring you here if he did. You mustn't tell him what I asked of you, should you choose to stay."

I exhale. "I told you I can't go with you."

"I aim to change your mind."

His admission causes more electricity and warmth. Too much is going on inside of me. I sit forward and move to the opposite side of the tub. The sheer size suggests it was meant for delicious activities for two. I stare at him from the other end of the tub. He picks up one of my feet and rubs his hands over it, offering pressure and caresses.

"You really are pretty," I say to him.

"No, you are."

"Maybe, but you really are. With your chiseled body and the perfect angles in your face. Your eyes are a color green I will never forget in a million years."

He blushes. "I could say the same of your particular shade of green."

"Hazel, they call it. Green with brown."

"Mesmerizing is what I call it."

My turn to blush. He presses into the arch of my foot and brings it close to his face. He licks my toe, and I tingle from head to toe. I pull my foot from his grasp and move forward and straddle him.

"Whitney, don't even think about it."

"What?" I tease.

"I didn't bring you here for sex. I brought you here to woo you."

I throw my head back in laughter. "You, men take and take, then flip the script." I rise up onto my knees and grab his cock into my hand. I position it where I need it to be and sink down on the delicious length. My eyes roll back at the feeling—the welcome fullness. When I open my eyes, he is staring at me in surprise. I don't move, and neither does he. We match each other stare for stare, and I realize in a crazy world I could love him. I think a sliver of my heart might.

His hands find my ass, and he squeezes, pressing me down further onto him.

I roll my hips, grinding his cock. Locking my eyes with his, he doesn't move a muscle. I rock back and forth and stare. I rise up and fall onto his long erection on repeat, never taking my eyes from his. He squeezes his eyes shut.

"Please open your eyes. If you are leaving me. I need this."

He obeys and smiles. His fingers dig into my ass, and I move harder, faster. Overcome by the weight of him leaving, I can't contain the sensations. They start in my chest, my belly, a tightening, and vibration—a hum. Then electricity and delicious aching numbness. My pussy contracts around him and I shake violently. The three words nearly spill out when he comes behind me, bringing my lips to his, spilling his essence inside of me. His cock contracting and swelling inside of me as he whispers the words in my ear and then takes my lips into his and doesn't let go.

We separate, my lips swollen, my body spent.

When we finally make it to the bed, dried and sated, I expect more. What I don't expect is for him to wrap me in his arms.

"I love you, Whitney."

I nod into his shoulder.

"You don't have to say anything. I think I already know."

He kisses the back of my head and neck, and we fall into a deep sleep.

The bright lights streaming into the room wake me hours later. I don't feel him. When I look around, he is gone.

12

WHITNEY

*N*o one is home when I wake up this morning. I think we have settled into our new normal, but no one can deny the brittleness in the air—as if the other shoe is destined to drop.

I plop myself on the floor in the center of my room and close my eyes just like I've done during meditation in therapy. We are focusing on pushing the thoughts and images of The Chamber out when they pop in; however, when a thought keeps pushing its way back, I must face it head on.

The imaginary waves roll towards me and recede over and over. I can hear them crashing, and I see the frothy bubbles and feel the coolness running through my toes. Briny, salty air assaults my nostrils. My body warms from the sun's brilliant rays. I breathe.

In through my nose, out through my mouth.

In through my nose, out through my mouth.

Thomas hissing in my face flashes before my eyes. I flinch. My heart begins to race.

In through my nose, out through my mouth.

I increase the size of my waves and they wash away the image.

My breathing is steady, my heart slows.

The ocean waves are replaced by a room so blindingly yellow that I can't see. I push the image back and grasp onto to my ocean. There is a mental battle between the ocean and the canary yellow room. I relent and let the image come into full focus.

I am sitting at the small bistro table. My sheer yellow dress clings to my body. Made up to look like a movie star, hair pressed into fine glossy sheets that fall down my back.

When the man enters my chamber he doesn't waste time on pleasantries. My yellow dress is a puddle on the floor around my feet. He tells me how beautiful I am and his entire length is inside of me before we make it to the bed. He smiles down at me, his tongue tasting my skin as he pulls his cock out and slams it back in over and over. He pulls out and spills his essence onto my skin.

My eyes fly open. I couldn't stay in that moment if I wanted to. Tears dampen my face. I let them fall. I'm trying, but as I look down at my shaking hands I know I've spent too much time there already. My therapist swears that with time I won't be so affected by it.

So, with blind faith, I complete the tasks she suggests I do for the sake of my therapy. Maybe Thomas is right. If I keep doing this, I shouldn't have to go to therapy anymore. I usually feel awful and spent after going there. Maybe if I increase my meditation I can do this by myself —one less person to look at me with eyes that wondered why I stayed, why I didn't fight. It could be all in my mind that they think this about me, but I don't think so. Even while we were inside, the other women and I discussed it. Could we successfully escape? But it always came back to our family. Mason demonstrated his power to us, and to leave there to find our families broken or worse would be adding guilt to the pain we had already suffered.

Going back and thinking about all the things I could have done differently is tearing me up just as bad as everything that has happened.

One thing I must admit to myself is that I was already on Mason's wish list two years prior. He would have found me anywhere. What ifs are so pointless, but they fill my mind, whether I want them too or not.

I attempt to close my eyes again. But this time the darkness is too loud. This session is most definitely over.

13

WHITNEY

*T*he past week has been tense—nightmares and relationships. Thomas and I haven't seen each other, but we have spoken daily. He doesn't ask, but I know he is waiting for an answer that I can't give him. With each thought of his desires and how out of alignment they are to mine, my insides knot and twist. *Can I do what he asks? Sleep with strangers for money? Is Thomas worth subjecting myself to such horrors?* The engagement ring on my finger feels like a noose. If I don't come up with a way to stop his plans, I either have to go along with them or risk losing him. My head hurts with all the ideas I have tried to come up with and failed.

Some genius.

The little voice in the back of my mind says I should just tell him about the money. Even a fraction of the four million would be more than enough help him and my family. But what does that voice know? If I did that we'd be together for sure. But I would always be the woman who got paid for sex, which is what he wants from me now. It would only prove to him that he was right to think I was perfect for the job. The shame would destroy me.

Fact is, Thomas can never know about the money. If I'm going to get him to agree to drop this horrific plan, I'll have to find another way. If he really loves me, he'll come to his senses. Only time will tell.

I shake the insanity from my head as arrive in the parking lot of the cafe. Today, I'm meeting Chalice for lunch, and I can't wait to see her. I miss her and Amaris so much. I haven't seen as much of my gals as I'd like; it seems while I was gone they went and got a life.

Amaris is in Europe modeling almost weekly. And Chalice has a job, an honest to goodness, five day a week job. When did we all grow up?

"Sweets," Chalice calls from a small table overlooking the ocean. She hops up from the table and wraps me in a Chalice-like hug—loving, with a little extra (what?) added in. I always thought she'd grow up and come out, but so far she hasn't. "So happy your dad lifted his embargo on your driving alone. You feel like a real adult now?" she teases.

I throw her a shady glare and then smile. She's right, I am happy with the extra freedom. "I'm starving," I announce, taking a seat opposite her. "This place is nice," I say and as I look around. The restaurant is more outdoors than in, with dark rustic wood support beams and heavy wooden floors. The tables and chairs bring the place to life with bright beige, blue, and salmon accents. There are pictures on all the walls, each photo is water related—ships, ocean, surfers, folks lazing about on the beach. The frames look handmade from recycled materials.

"What was here before?" I ask Chalice. I certainly can't remember. I've only been to this beach a couple of times. This area is trendy and too busy for the taste of most of us locals who want a relaxing day.

"There used to be a dessert shop here, remember?" Chalice asks.

I think for a second, and let out a long, "Oh, I do remember." I take another look around. "You got a good table." I glance out over the water. I will never get enough of it.

"You know it. And I ordered for us, fish and chips and two daiquiris each."

I feign exaggerated excitement. "Thank you. I'm starving."

Chalice sits back in her seat and watches me. Waiting.

"What?" I ask. I have no plans to tell her about Thomas' new money-making scheme. I stare at her with the same goofy smile on my face that she has plastered across hers.

She shakes her head at me. "Show me the damn ring, already."

Oh that. I laugh at her. I'd forgotten I was wearing it or that I told her about it.

Chalice squeals, nearly ripping my arm off when she pulls my hand closer to her face. "He ain't cheap, that's for sure. This set him back."

Oh dear lord, I hope not. Thomas has enough financial woes. I give her my fakest smile.

She releases my hand after studying each stone with the eye of an experienced jeweler, which she is not. She sits back in her seat and the smile on her face tells me that she is happy for me. The waitress sets two glasses of water in front of us and tells us our cocktails and food will be arriving shortly. I take a few sips of the cool water.

"So, I was thinking we could have a double wedding," she says, then pauses and jumps with the excitement of something better from the look in her eyes. I know when Chalice is cooking up a scheme. "Or maybe a back-to-back wedding. Same location. The guests can sit in one spot for both ceremonies. We'd have neutral decorations with the pop of color coming from each of our wedding parties." Chalice continues rattling on about our co-wedding.

"Wait." I lean forward. "Are you getting married? To who?"

She waves me off. "I'm dating a handsome fellow from America, sweets. It's long distance, but he knows what a catch I am. I figure he'll pop that all important question any day now."

"You are so crazy, Chalice. I'm not even thinking about weddings—"

Suddenly, I'm cut off by a familiar form standing near our table. "Nikolai?"

"Whitney? I thought that was you. How've you been?"

His eyes zero in on the ring on my finger. I slide my hand under the table and feel my cheeks warm with embarrassment. My hand suddenly feels the weight of the ring magnified. I know what he's thinking, and he has it all wrong. I haven't done anything for Thomas, and if I have my way I won't have to. I've been trying to work out a way to tell him about the money, or that I've come into some money—not millions. I just haven't figured out how yet.

"I'm being so rude. Nikolai, this is my best friend, Chalice. Chalice this is my—" My mind runs through how to introduce him. I can't say that he is the man who paid Thomas to sleep with me, but graciously let me out of the deal. "—um, friend, Nikolai. We know each other from my trauma group," I lie. The lies are starting to pile up because I stopped going to group. However, my friends and family don't know that.

They shake hands. "I had no idea there were men that look like this in your group. Hell, I'd go too," Chalice says, being Chalice.

Nikolai laughs politely at her comment.

"Chalice, give me a second. I need to talk to Nikolai about something," I say. I turn to him, "You have a minute?"

His smile makes my heart stutter. I feel the intensity and magnitude of depth beyond that smile.

"For you? Of course." He turns to walk out of the small bistro, gesturing for me to lead the way, and he follows me.

"Don't be long, or I'm gonna drink your drink, both of them." Chalice calls out to me.

Nikolai and I make our way down a sidewalk that separates the sand from the parking lot.

We continue in silence until we are in a less-crowded area, and he takes a seat on an empty bench. I look around and make sure I'm not breaking Daddy's rules. There are plenty of people within screaming distance, and I wouldn't have to scream loud. The only place he could take me is to the sandy beach or the parking lot. When I feel a bit more relaxed, I take the seat next to him.

I don't look at him, instead I stare out at the water. I don't know this man, but for some reason, unknown to me, I feel the need to clear the air with him. "It's not what you think," I say.

He follows suit and keeps his gaze focused on the water. If he is anything like me, he could get lost for hours in the soothing rhythm of the waves. "Please explain. Because I remember the last time we spoke, I encouraged you to get away from Thomas and all the mess he comes with, and now you have his ring on your finger. That looks like the opposite of heeding my warning."

I sigh. *Why does this man even care? I'm a stranger to him.* "He's different. I don't know, less desperate. He hasn't asked me to do anything since that night. I told him I needed more time, and he's giving it to me." I dare a glance up at him.

He stares back. His eyebrows slide up his face. "So, you're planning on doing it?" he asks.

"Absolutely not. But I need time to figure out a way to get him to change his mind."

"So, you didn't tell him that we didn't really do anything?"

"No," I mumble.

"Why?"

I shrug my shoulders. I am exhausted from explaining myself to people. Everyone wants answers to questions that I haven't had time to think about yet. I'm still trying to figure out who the hell I am now. The girl I was before would have dropped Thomas in a heartbeat. No, the girl I was before would be someone Thomas would never have asked. I'm not the only one who doesn't recognize myself anymore—no one else does either.

"He's not the only guy for you, Whitney. The right guy is out there."

This guy sees right through me, pulling my fears right from my head. "He's all I have. He knows what I went through and he still wants me."

Nikolai takes in a couple of deep breaths; he doesn't speak. Instead he turns his attention back to the water. I don't feel anything negative bristling from him, nothing simmering below the surface. Just calm. It takes over me, too. I steal a couple of glances at him while we share this silence. I don't know what he's thinking.

Nikolai looks so much younger than the first time I saw him. The lighting in the hotel room wasn't bright enough for me to make out his features fully. Now in navy board shorts and a fitted tee that reveals how much time he must spend at the gym, he can't be in his thirties, late twenties at best. His eyes are lighter than I originally thought, blue-gray. He is downright, deliciously handsome, with the perfect amount of fullness to his moist lips, and a thick mess of tousled dark brown hair.

I wait for him to speak because I have nothing else to say.

"Look, I know we don't know each other. And our first encounter was, *unique.* But please explain to me why you feel Thomas is the only one who will love you."

I take a moment to think about the answer. *How much of my inner weakness do I really want this man to know? How much more, I should say?* "Look, Nikolai—"

"Niko, please," he corrects me.

"Niko. I know what I am. What I've become. He knows my darkest secret, my pain, and he wants me anyway. Who else will?"

"That's not true and you know it. That's fear talking."

"Maybe it is. But fear is a hell of an emotion," I say as I look down. "He proposed to me and gave me a ring; that has to mean something."

Unease lines his features. "I'm not here to squash your dreams or happiness, but he is a bad guy. He is preying on your fears right now. What happened to you is unspeakable. But for him to say he loves you and not protect you, and ask you do more of the same is worse. I know you're stronger than that. Get out while you can."

I flinch as if he slapped me with his hand instead of harsh words. This man doesn't even know me. I jump up from the bench.

"Wait." He jumps up too. "I shouldn't have said that. It's just, I haven't stopped thinking about you since that night—worrying about you. I know you don't know me, but I see you, Whitney. You are a beautiful and strong woman—much stronger than you believe yourself to be—and you deserve better than him, than this."

I exhale the breath I was holding, sit back down and Niko follows. He isn't the enemy; for some reason, this man cares for me. "You sound a lot like my therapist with all your *I'm so strong* and *what I deserve* business. But I'm a smart girl, and I see me too. I'm damaged goods. That place took everything away from me. I don't talk about it with my family, but I'm frightened all the time. I have sickening nightmares, even when I'm awake." The tears fall and I don't even stop them. "What sane man will want to have anything to do with the baggage I come with?" There is no sense hiding from Niko. He sees my truth better than anyone, even if he found it by accident. "What if...what if Thomas is exactly what I deserve?"

Niko looks hurt by my words. "You should listen to your therapist. Just because you have all those book smarts in your head doesn't mean you know and see everything clearly."

I sigh. "Point taken. But I stopped therapy. So, I guess I don't have to bother with how she saw me."

Niko's expression tells me he is not pleased about me quitting. "Why?"

"I have Thomas now. He said therapy is for the weak; he believes— just like you do—that I'm strong. I don't know if I believe it myself. I just want to feel normal again." I wipe the tears trickling down my cheeks. "You see, Niko, you don't have to worry about me."

He reaches for my hand but stops inches away and pulls back. "Whitney, I'm begging you. Get away from him. He doesn't deserve you. Get back into therapy. Thomas will use you and leave you. Trust me, I know his type. You deserve a man who will help you, not take from you. You deserve happiness."

I stand up again. This man is as crazy as he is attractive. I continue to wipe my tears as his words fill me with sadness. "I gave up on fairytales, Niko. They're for dreamers, and when I close my eyes, all I have are nightmares. Prince Charming just doesn't exist, not for me. Thanks for the pep talk. I know you mean well. You seem like a great guy." I turn and start walking back towards the restaurant.

"Hey, Whitney," Niko calls after me. I turn toward him. We lock eyes and a moment passes by before he speaks, though his eyes speak volumes. "You still have my card?"

I nod.

"Use it." He smiles at me. "And I'm not giving up. I'm gonna check on you again, now that you have me worried about you."

I shake my head in amusement and can't wipe the smile from my face. He meets my eyes and stares. His smile warms me as it takes over his entire face, meeting his blue eyes.

"Okay, Niko," I say and turn to walk away again. I can feel him watching me. Then a thought hits me and I turn back to him.

"Hey, Niko. If you do find him, send him my way; I'd be interested in a chat."

He raises his eyebrows in question. "Him who?"

"The amazing guy you spoke of." This time I turn away for good, and I'd swear I hear him say *I'm right here*. But that can't be. Ocean breezes have a way of playing tricks on you. But, I'd be lying if I didn't wish it were true.

14

NIKO

*N*ever would I have imagined a woman so amazing could feel so bad about herself that she would hitch her wagon to such a loser. All I can do for now is watch Whitney walk away. But I won't be far. Until I gain her trust, I will watch her from afar and arrange the occasional bump into each other. There is no way I'm going to let Thomas use her. She has been through enough this last year of her life, and even though she doesn't see her worth, I do, and no way am I letting a snake like Thomas ruin her further.

I wish she could see herself the way I do—smart and gorgeous. I watch her walk away until she disappears inside of the restaurant and one thought enters my mind before I can stop it, *I hope she calls.* This isn't about me and her, no matter how attracted I am to this woman. This is about stopping this low-level thug before he becomes a powerful madman. And this is about making sure that I keep him away from Whitney.

I know just where to start. I pull my phone out of my pocket and shoot a text to Thomas to arrange a meet up.

I PULL up to Milo's an hour later.

"Milo, how's it going?" I greet the owner of the boxing gym.

He extends his hand out to mine and shakes it. "Niko, I'm doing just fine for an old man," he says.

Milo was a great boxer back in his day. He's deep into his seventies now, but he never misses a workout.

"Thomas back there yet?" I ask.

"Not yet, but I'll send him your way as soon as he shows up, unless you want another sparring partner." Milo throws a punch combination into the air.

I shake my head. "I'm not ready for you, Milo." I tease.

"Smart man," he says and pats my back.

I make my way to one of the practice rings, drop my bag, and run through a quick warm up. Jumping rope, shadow boxing, and ab work. Thomas appears a few minutes later and joins me in the warm up. He doesn't miss a beat, dropping to pushups matching my pace. When we finish warming up, we enter the ring.

"You ready for me?" he asks while he slips his hands into his gloves.

"Always." I want to ask him about business, but it's better if I let him bring it up.

We touch gloves in the center of the ring. I have a half-foot on him in height and a good forty or more pounds, but Thomas is scrappy. He throws a couple of jabs that I block and counter with a flurry of my own. When I look at him, I don't just see a petty criminal just starting out. Now I see a monster in the making. A man so reckless and selfish he would hurt anyone to get what he wants.

Thomas and I dance around the ring, punching, blocking, trading impressive flurries and combinations. "So, you think you could help me out with another date with my girl?" Thomas asks, dancing around the ring.

I feign ignorance. "You mean the hottie from the other night?"

"Yeah, I'm putting some things together, and soon I should have a couple more ladies lined up. But she's gonna be my star. If you have trustworthy friends, maybe you could send them my way? I'm ready to grow this venture," he says and throws a series of body shots that hit me in the side and abs.

I don't say anything at first, just continue boxing, returning the body blows.

When we're both significantly winded, him more than me, we leave the ring and head to a nearby bench. I use my towel to dry myself off. Then I replenish the water I lost. I turn to Thomas, resisting the urge to smash his face with my fist. "Man, I'm down. But that chick from the other day, she didn't seem like much of a pro."

Thomas laughs. "Nah, she's not, but she'll come around." He covers his head with his towel and lies down on the bench.

I take the opportunity to glare at him. Monster in the making. I break the stare before I get caught. "Yeah, whatever you say. Like I said, I'll help you out again, and I'll see if I have some boys that would be interested."

Thomas sits up. "That's what I'm talking about. Only people you trust though. I can't have any fucking cops getting wind of this before I get my business off the ground."

I stand and grab my bag. "Nah, we don't want that shit," I say. "That was a good workout." I point at him. "Make sure you hydrate or you'll be sore. I'm gonna get home and shower."

Thomas hops up from the bench and shakes my hand. "Thanks. Same time next week?"

"You got it."

I leave Thomas and head for the exit. I say goodbye to Milo and head to my truck, the whole time thinking what a piece of shit Thomas really is. He cares about nothing but himself. Whitney is not safe. His mind is set on making her a pawn in his game. No, not a pawn, the pawn—which means she is not safe. A guy that desperate would hurt her to get what he wants.

15

WHITNEY

"*Sunshine, I knew you would fall asleep in your Chamber sooner or later,*" *Montclair says waking me up. I can feel the bed depress under his weight. When I open my eyes, I'm confused, disoriented, and shocked that I fell asleep. I had made it months without falling asleep. After hours of sex, the last thing I want is my personal guard getting to take his turn with me. "I have been waiting for this for months. Rules are rules, so I hope you have as much fun as I know I will," he says.*

I rub my eyes to wake myself up and really see him for the first time. "I fell asleep?"

"You sure did, now why don't you get over here and wrap those sweet little lips around my cock," he says.

I do as he asks. My jaws not fully recovered from earlier. Montclair's penis isn't huge, thankfully, but I wouldn't call him small either. He lays on his back and I kneel over him and take him into my mouth and suck him, hard. The sooner I wear him out the sooner I can go back to my room. But he stops me before he comes. He repositions me on all fours and gets behind me. He slips inside of me. "You like that?"

"Yes, yes," I lie. I have learned how to fake the feeling.

Montclair thrusts in and out of me fast and hard. I can hear him breathing behind me, I know it won't be long. I'm relieved when he spills inside of me, his body going rigid, shaking behind me. "That's not all, I got more in me. You might not ever fall asleep again, and I came to play. He flips me over onto my back, my legs over his shoulders and he sinks inside of me again. His face so close to mine and all I can think is please don't kiss me. When he does I want to throw up in my mouth and die. He continues to kiss me, while he thrusts himself deep inside of me....

Like most nights that I dream, my screams are what wake me. My family stopped bursting into my room weeks ago, hearing my screams rattle through the house is something their bodies have adapted to. It used to scare them to death, but I explained it to them how Dr. Wesley explained it to me—it's part of my process and the dreams will ebb in time.

My face is wet. The last thing I want to do is go back there. I pick up my phone and turn on the flashlight to see what I'm looking for. I find it on my bedside table, the business card. I punch in the numbers and don't realize that it could be three a.m. until after the phone starts ringing. Before I make the decision to hang up a gruffy voice answers. I definitely woke him up.

"Hello?" his voice sends warmth, flooding me for reasons I can't explain. He isn't mine. I barely know this man.

"Hi. I'm sorry to call so late."

"Whitney?"

"Should I let you get back to sleep? I didn't realize the time."

I can hear him moving around through the phone. "No, it's fine. It's not that late. Wait, it's one in the morning. Are you sure you're okay?"

I can hear genuine concern in his voice. Maybe I made a mistake. I shouldn't bring him into my mess. "I'm sorry, Niko, I shouldn't have woken you. Have a good night," I say and end the call. I set my phone on my night stand and stare into the dark void.

I don't know if it is a gift or a curse that we can't see into the future, not even a flash of our life ten minutes from now. Yet we plan and schedule the future, never knowing what is lurking around the corner.

My phone begins vibrating.

"Hello," I say into the receiver knowing that it's Niko.

"Why'd you hang up? I told you it was okay. I promise. You can call me anytime."

"But why?"

There's a pause. "Because you wouldn't have called if you didn't need me, and I'm a sucker for a beautiful woman in need." I can hear the smile on his face.

"Ha, ha, ha."

Niko laughs in response. "Seriously, what's keeping you up tonight?" he asks. His voice is velvety smooth and comforts me.

I sigh. "What isn't?" I pause and Niko doesn't push. "I had a bad dream," I say with a sigh.

"You wanna tell me about it?" he asks.

I pull the covers over me and settle deeper within my bed. "Not really. I just don't wanna be alone in the dark right now. We can talk about anything you want."

Niko yawns. It's one of those long, exaggerated yawns that relieves tension from your body. "Okay, tell me about yourself. Like how'd you get to be so smart?"

An easy question. This makes me smile. I lie back onto my pillow and pull the covers to my chin. "I just always was. When other kids were learning to read, I was doing algebra and reading classic literature. Being smart has always been the norm for me. It made things hard for me socially, especially with boys my age."

"I bet. I'm a grown man, and I'm intimidated by you."

"Oh, stop teasing. You handle yourself very well," I say and then add, "I mean, for someone of normal intelligence."

We both laugh at that. Talking to Niko, I'm starting to feel more relaxed. "My turn," I say.

"Ask me anything."

"How old are you?" I ask.

"Take a guess."

I'm such a bad guesser of age. Luckily, with men guessing younger is not the compliment it is with women. With a woman it's about looks, but with a man it's about maturity. "Twenty-seven?" I take a stab.

"Close. I'm twenty-eight."

"Okay. Where are you from, because you don't sound like an islander?"

"My mother is British and my father is Greek. I was born in London, but raised mostly in America. I have citizenship in America, England, and Greece. I've lived in all three places at some point in my life, hence the accent. How about you? Because you definitely sound like an islander."

To this I laugh. "Through and through. But I'm ready to see other places." My smile grows at the possibilities other places might bring. "Do you like living on the island?" I ask him.

"You can say it's growing on me. But me, I could live anywhere."

Our conversation goes on for hours. I learn that Niko is an Aries, loves all things beach and water, has an older sister and a younger brother. He moved here after his sister did, and he has a husky named Dreamer. I also learn that he is very worried about me. We even fell asleep a couple of times. I love that our conversation remained clear of painful topics or people. When the sun came up, we decided it was time to end the call and start our days.

It was some night. The best I've had in eons.

TODAY I PLAN to reach out to University College to discuss continuing my education. I send an email to the admissions office, telling them that I am alive and kicking and would love to begin my doctoral program in the fall. I include all of my relevant information and hit send. My phone pings an alert just as I finish.

Niko: *Hey there, Whittie. Are you half asleep like I am?*

Me: *I should have never told you my nickname. That so better not stick. It took years for me to shake it.*

Niko: *But it's perfect! I'm in desperate need of coffee. You want to meet me somewhere?*

I stare at the screen. A late-night phone call that lasted into the wee hours and now coffee?

Niko: *?*

I can't see the harm, and I could definitely use another friend, especially this one.

Me: *Sure.*

He sends me an address to a coffee shop on the beach. I know the shop. It's on a section of beach that is less crowded. I won't lead Niko on, all though my body is rocked with excitement.

I throw on a pair of denim cut off shorts, a royal blue tank, and sandals. I bump into my father on my way out.

"Where you headed, pumpkin?"

I give him a peck on the cheek and a hug. "Meeting a friend at the beach for coffee."

"Grab a hat, the news reported that the UV would be brutal today."

Always the parent. I shake my head at him and grab a big floppy straw hat from the coat rack that we use for every style of hat imaginable. I place it on my head. "You know this is going to ruin my curls," I say and roll my eyes at my father, but I give him a smile before I turn and walk out the door.

When I make it to the coffee shop, Niko is easy to spot. He's sitting at a small table facing the water. His gaze is lost in the waves. I stop, feigning searching for something in my purse. But really, I'm giving myself a chance to calm my beating heart that is threatening to break free from my chest. After a few deep breaths, I make my way towards my very attractive friend. He's wearing a fitted gray tee and colorful board shorts.

"Hey," I say walking up to the table.

Niko hops up and surprises me with a hug. His scent is a subtle mint and lavender, with a hint of the sea. Whatever he is wearing smells divine on him. I melt into his arms if only for a second; it feels good to be here. "I'm glad you could make it," he says.

I pull my hat from my head and muss my hair so that it isn't flat. "I would have ordered for you but in our conversation last night, I mean this morning, we never discussed coffee," Niko says.

I blush. "Well. I like a lot of milk in my coffee. I take my coffee about my skin tone."

Niko smiles at me and then laughs. He is really attractive. I've never had a male friend that was this good-looking *and* straight. My lord, he is hard to look away from.

"What? Can you let me in on the joke," I say and begin to laugh too, even though I have no idea what I'm actually laughing at.

"Milk in the coffee? Dark and light? Are you sure you prefer a lot of milk?" he teases.

"Ha, ha. I get it. You, sir, are a dork." I glance up at him and he has stopped laughing, and so have I. We lock eyes with each other. Mine saying: *Where did you come from? We are definitely crossing a line. This feels a whole lot more like a date than coffee amongst friends.*

Thankfully, a waitress comes and takes our order. "The lady will have a cup of your strongest roast with enough creamer to match her gorgeous complexion." He looks at me and stuns me with his pure smile. I blush in return.

"And for you?" the waitress asks.

"I take mine black."

I start coughing until my eyes water. "You really are a dork." I shake my head at him, smiling until my cheeks hurt.

"Hey, I like what I like."

I ignore his comment. "Any exciting plans today?" I ask.

"More exciting than spending time with you?"

I roll my eyes at him, but smile. "If I didn't know better, I'd think you were throwing your hat into the ring, sir?"

Niko shrugs. "Whatever could you mean?"

"I'm a prodigy, remember, loads of smarts up here." I point to my head. "You think you stand a chance?" I tease.

"I do," he says.

"What about this?" I hold up my ring finger with Thomas' ring on it.

The waitress brings our coffees and sets the mugs in front of us. I quickly add two sugars to mine and take a sip. It is rich and creamy, just the way I like it. I look up at Niko and give him a satisfied smile. I guess he'd forgotten all about my fiancé.

"Looks heavy."

That wasn't what I was expecting him to say. "Funny, sometimes it is difficult to lift my arm," I tease. But there is more truth to my words. It does feel heavy with uncertainty and the lies I tell myself.

We sip our coffee in silence, staring out at the sea. Niko has stunned the words right out of me. He is the one person I can't lie to. He knows my truth, my shame, and he sits across the table from me with a genuine smile.

He knows what Thomas asked of me. He even knows what I endured in The Chamber, at least to some extent, and yet he is here offering me his friendship. Still, he is a stranger and Thomas is, well, he's not. Sure, recently he has shown me a side of him that I didn't know existed, but I also know that any one of us would surprise even ourselves with doing unimaginable things if backed into dark enough corner.

Thomas is a proud man that has lost everything. I can see it was desperation that drove him to his actions, and I have to believe in my heart that he otherwise would never have placed me in the middle of this craziness. Which means if I can get him to see reason, he may change his mind and we can put this behind us.

"Can we talk about last night?" Niko breaks into my thoughts.

"What about it?" I ask, looking into his eyes.

"The nightmare."

I stare into his eyes. "I don't want to talk about it."

He sits back in his chair. "As your new friend, I think you need to talk to somebody. It doesn't have to be me. But since you quit therapy—" He looks down and then up at me again, letting the words hang. "— which I think was a bad idea, you have to get that shit out. It isn't healthy. Do you talk to Thomas about what happened?"

I shake my head. *He'd probably take notes for his business.* "Can't I just pretend it never happened?"

It's his turn to shake his head. He leans forward on the table and takes one of my hands. "Are you still scared?"

He is so heading down a path I don't want any parts of. I don't miss therapy one bit. Talking about what happened to me is excruciating. Sure, the dreams are horrible, but talking about it is the equivalent of getting a full body wax. And that doesn't even include the judgy looks, or the question on everyone's mind: *why didn't you try and escape*? "Yes."

"And we both know you're having bad dreams."

I nod.

"Then it's consuming you, which means you're not doing a good job at pretending or forgetting, Whitney." He pauses and watches me. "At least think about going back into therapy."

My eyes mist with tears. I look into Niko's eyes and his expression makes the tears fall. He is really worried about me. He gets up from his seat and moves his chair closer to mine. He opens his arms out to me, and I fall into them without hesitation.

"I promise if you face this shit, you can get through it. I'm hear if you want to talk about anything. Ever. Okay?"

I nod my head against his muscular chest. He doesn't attempt to move until I do.

"Thank you," I say, softly breaking contact with him and blotting my eyes with a napkin. If I didn't know any better I'd think he was a therapist. He talks like one, one who swears. "Can I ask you a question?"

"Anything."

"Where'd you come from?"

I don't need to clarify. He knows exactly what I mean. Part of me wonders if he is being so nice because he feels sorry for me. My phone pings with an alert, interrupting our moment. When I turn it on I see a text from Thomas, not asking, but telling me that he's picking me up for dinner this week. Strange I get nothing from the message, no butterflies in my stomach or excitement over the idea of seeing him.

"What's wrong?" Niko asks.

"Nothing. Just a text from your competition," I tease. "You know, the one who put the ring on my finger."

"You don't look very happy about that."

I sit back in my seat. "I know. I just. He wants me to pencil him in for dinner this week." I shrug. It's difficult to explain. "He hasn't brought anything up about his business, but still, it's like this giant silent elephant in the room when we're together. Like I'm waiting for him to bring it up, while secretly hoping he never does."

"Have you figured out how to change his mind?"

"Nope," I sigh.

"So, tell him you have plans," Niko says with a sly smile.

"He's my fiancé; I can't turn him down." I smile at Niko, but it's brittle.

I know Niko means well. I know he wants me to be this strong woman, but I don't think I can be the woman he wants me to be, and I definitely can't be the woman Thomas wants me to be. I don't even know who I want me to be. The old me was carefree and fun loving, smart but never cocky about it. The old me loved laughing until I nearly peed myself, and planning for the future. This me can barely plan for the next day.

"I'd better get going, Niko. Thanks for the coffee and the chat. You're really a good listener."

Niko tosses money onto the table and follows me out. We walk toward my car in silence.

"Hey, I've been meaning to ask you about your tattoo," I say and point toward his forearm. He has a drawing of a person fishing, but instead of a large body of water, it's a fish tank, with a gold fish on the line.

"This old thing." He looks down at his arm.

"A joke of sorts."

I look at him and nod. "Okay."

His response is a light laugh that causes butterflies to crowd my stomach.

He opens my car door when we reach it, and I give him a hug before I get in. I don't even think about it, I just do it. My head rests on his chest, and if things were different in my life, if I wasn't already engaged to someone, Niko would definitely the type of guy I would fall for.

"Hey, don't hesitate to call me for any reason."

"You too," I say, and his smile grows.

Niko waves when I pull out of the parking space. On the way home, my brain starts putting the two men into categories. Thomas' good qualities: smart, handsome, ambitious, somewhat romantic. His bad qualities: his ambition and his desire to use me to make money.

Then there's Niko, who seriously came out of nowhere. He's smart, handsome, caring, and very romantic. I'm sure he has negatives, but he hasn't shown them to me yet.

Why couldn't I have met Niko first?

16

NIKO

*W*hitney is a stunning woman, and it kills me that she is so broken that she doesn't even know it. Women that look like her and have accomplished as much as she has usually possess a confidence to match, but a lot of hers was stolen from her. But I believe she is strong enough to reclaim it. I believe she is strong enough to do anything she sets her mind to.

When I look into her eyes I can see the pain she tries to hide from everyone—even herself. She doesn't even know how brave she is, and I hope I'm around when she realizes it.

I am so fortunate. I get to see her in a way that no one else does. Not her parents, not her friends, and certainly not Thomas. I get to see her truth. It's the gift she keeps hidden from her loved ones so they don't worry. After everything she's been through, her thoughts are for their wellbeing and not her own. She doesn't see her strength the way that I do, yet.

Once Whitney is no longer in sight, I turn to my truck, stopping to reach into my pocket and answer my phone. "Andres," I say into my phone.

"It's Sam," my partner says on the other end. "You sounded stressed on your message. You're never stressed; what gives?"

"I broke protocol, and I need your help."

Sam gives me the expected reaction when she bursts into laughter. All I can do is wait for her to shut the hell up so that I can speak. This shit must be really funny because she is still going strong when I hop into my truck.

"You done, or are you done?"

She stops abruptly. "You're serious?"

"Dead serious."

"Which regulation? You never break protocol, Niko. What happened? What'd you do, go out there and get sun poisoning in the tropics? Need some London fog?"

I slam my truck door and squeeze my eyes shut. She is right. I never break the rules. "Number two." I admit and wait for the shit storm she will most likely rain down on me, payback for the shit I've given her over the span of our partnership.

"Seriously? You got involved with a perp? Wait, isn't the perp a dude?"

"No, not the perp, Sam. His fiancé. And we're not involved, but I like her—too much. I need your help because I don't think I can be objective where she is concerned. I mean, I want to save her more than I want to bring the perp down."

There is silence on the phone that I want to break but don't. I have no idea what Sam is doing, but I know we still have a connection because I can hear her shuffling around.

"Just booked my flight. I'll see you tomorrow."

"Thanks, Sam," I say and hang up the phone.

Okay, maybe now I can get back on track. Sam will know what to do. I know she'll give me some shit, but not too much because I have bailed her out too many times. I live by the rules, always have. But not Sam; she uses them as more of a guide—a very loose guide.

"There she is," I say aloud to myself and wrap Sam in a huge bear hug. "My hero," I tease.

"Okay, okay, hero here. Get off me, you big oaf," she says. She pushes me away, always uncomfortable with affection of any type.

I let go and take in my partner. I was so excited for her to come and bail me out of this shit that I didn't even see all that she had going on —the long blond hair, nearly to her waist; so much makeup; a short fitted candy pink dress; and sky-high pink heels.

I burst out into laughter.

"What? This job requires a hooker. I don't look the bloody part?"

I keep laughing and pull at her blonde hair.

"Sure. All you need is chewing gum, and you'll be the prototypical hooker." I shake my head at Sam; she doesn't do shit halfway, that's for sure. "Come on." I grab her bags and toss them into the backseat of my truck and climb into the driver's seat.

"What?" she says, slamming her door closed. She knows I hate it when she slams the door. I give her what she wants and cut my eyes at her.

"This working girl has a job to do."

I continue laughing as I pull into traffic.

"Too much?"

"Yes, a bit."

"Huh. I'll tell you what's too much, this bloody sun. How can you even open your eyes all the way?" she whines as she squints.

"Seven months of sunglasses," I say, "but, damn that get up. Less is more around here. You look like some big city call girl. Your vibe is more reality television when it should be low-key, island time."

"So, what you're saying is?"

"Dial it back, way back."

We continue down the highway toward her hotel.

"I was wondering why everyone on the plane was staring. I wanted to shout, haven't you guys ever seen a hooker before."

All I can do is smile and shake my head at my partner. "How you ever survived doing undercover is beyond me."

"Ha. I'm amazing at this shit cause I'm real."

"Whatever. I checked you into a hotel. As far as your origin goes, you're my cousin from America."

She smiles. "I do a great American accent. Can I be from California?" she asks, sounding like she just flew in from SoCal. "I guess I can lose these itchy things. "She begins unclipping blonde hair pieces until she has a pile in her lap. Then she reaches into her purse and goes to work wiping the makeup from her face. When she's done, she exhales as if the whole charade was a heavy chore.

"Hey, there's my partner," I tease.

"Ha, ha, ha." She does the ugly face that goes so well with her sarcastic laugh, while she twists her shoulder length blonde hair into a pile on top of her head. Thomas doesn't stand a chance.

She slaps her hands together, throws her feet on my dash and reclines her seat. "What's the plan?"

She really is real. This is her all the time, relaxed and comfortable in her own skin. She once told me that she came to be an international crime task force agent when her sister was killed by her boyfriend. He was such a sociopath, no one suspected him for nearly a year before he slipped up. She has been on a mission ever since.

She and I came up with the term, SF, "little fish or small fish" together. It drives other agents crazy. But we don't care.

My story is a little different. I was a runt for the longest time. In middle school, I looked like I could be in elementary school, and during my freshman year, I could have been a sixth grader. Bullies took advantage of my size. I was an easy target. It became a sport for them, but I was determined to overcome my situation. I asked my folks to put me in a self-defense course, and they did. I began taking jujitsu, Krav Maga, and wrestling. By the end of 10th grade, I was no longer their target. Come to find out, I was a late bloomer. I was five-eight by the end of 10th grade, and when I returned to school in 11th grade, I was five-eleven.

I had a new mission, because as bullies often do, mine found a new target. My job was to protect the smaller kids from the same fate. Bullies usually fly under the radar—they never seem to get caught doing their shit. I developed a watch group that kept an eye on bullies. Most of the members in the group were from my wrestling team and my girlfriend who was cheerleader captain. The school still has the watch group to this day. The principal even started a program to help bullies, too, because some of them were lashing out because of problems at home. I've gone back and spoken about cyber bullying and helped them develop a watch team for that as well. The administration does annual incentives and bullying is at an all-time low.

When this case is over, I plan to work more in schools, developing similar bully-free programs. But for now, I have to deal with this tiny bottom feeder I have on my hook.

"The plan: I'm going to introduce you to Thomas at the gym tomorrow, and you can work your magic. Please tell me you didn't just bring Barbie clothes."

She sticks her tongue out at me. "I brought normal clothes too, you wanker."

I wipe my forehead in exaggerated relief.

"Now tell me all about this island girl that has you all twisted up."

I fill her in on everything that has happened so far, including the biggest concern I have as I escort her to her room. I want to know if she believes Whitney will forgive me when she finds out who I really am.

After entering the room, Sam goes straight to the window and yanks the curtains back revealing her ocean view.

"Smashing view isn't it? I think I'm getting sun sick already. You'd have to go crazy with this much bloody sun day in and day out."

I shrug. "You get used to it."

We chat about tomorrow, and I tell her what she should wear as I head for the door. Before I walk through it, I turn to her and say, "Sam, thank you so much for coming."

She smirks. "Are you kidding? You don't break the rules. I knew you needed me pretty bad. She's a lucky girl. I hope she gets a chance to see that."

All I can do is look down. "And what about the lie?"

"I mean. You can't help the circumstances in which you and she met. It'll work out in the end, you'll see."

"You're probably right. See you tomorrow."

It feels strange being the rule breaker for once in this partnership, but in my defense, I never saw Whitney coming.

17

NIKO

Thomas is warming up when I enter the training session. Now that I know the stakes, I regret training him. In the last seven months, he has become faster and stronger, which is an undesirable combination for Whitney. But he and I started this journey before I knew what he was capable of. Bad business deals are one thing, prostitution is another.

"Hey, man," he says when I drop my bag.

I nod instead of speak.

"You good?" he asks.

"Me? Yeah. Just up late. My cousin, Sam, came in from California late last night and couldn't sleep, so that meant I had to stay up and entertain. Hey, you don't mind if my cousin watches or works out with us? I can charge you the group rate instead of private."

"It's all good," Thomas says. "Besides, it'll give me someone else's ass to kick for a change," he says.

This arrogant fucker. "Ha. I mean you do know, I've been taking it easy on you, right?"

Thomas laughs. "Whatever you say."

This doesn't even need a reply. "I thought we'd focus on some injury prevention while we wait for Sam."

Thomas climbs through the ropes and joins me on a mat. We begin with a series of stretches.

"Did I miss the workout?" Sam's familiar voice rings through the air.

I hop up from the floor. "You made it," I say and give her a hug. "Sam, this is Thomas; Thomas, my cousin, Sam."

Thomas looks back and forth between us in disbelief. "*This* is your cousin? I thought she was a guy. Sam's a guy's name."

We both laugh at Thomas' reaction.

"Yep, but it's a lot easier to say and spell, than Jessamine. Nice to meet you, Thomas."

I watch as Thomas checks my partner out from head to toe; he is more than pleased with what he sees. Sam is decked out in tight workout pants and a sports bra, her blonde hair in a ponytail.

"Let's get back to stretching," I say and know that Sam is about to reel him in.

She ignores our hamstring stretch and jumps into a series of splits in all directions, followed by spreading her legs out wide and flattening her torso to the floor. She looks over at Thomas and smiles, while he gawks.

My partner has a way with men. She oozes a natural sensuality that she yields like a weapon. Rare men can see passed it without getting trapped in her snare. I'm one of the rare ones who can. Sam and I are the truest example of how the opposite sex can be friends. We never once considered a romantic entanglement. She always joked that we're both too pretty. But then how would you explain Whitney who is every bit as gorgeous as Sam?

Part of it for me is being a natural protector; Sam never needed protecting. It isn't that I see her as one of the guys—more like a sister that kicked my ass and defended me growing up—like siblings.

Thomas doesn't stand a chance.

"I'll be right back," I say, but neither of them even acknowledges me.

I head to the men's locker room and shoot a text to Whitney.

Me: *Hey, just checking up on you. How're you doing?*

Whitney: *I'm hanging out with my family at the beach. What're you doing?*

Me: *Working out. Sorry I didn't call you yesterday. My cousin came into town. I'd love for you guys to meet.*

Whitney: *You don't have to apologize.*

Me: *I'd like to see you. Check on you in person.*

Whitney: *I'd like that too. Enjoy your workout.*

The smile on my face makes my cheeks hurt. I really like this girl. When I return to the workout area, Sam and Thomas are flirting just as I suspected.

"Hey, hey. Did I forget to mention that my cousin has a boyfriend, and Thomas here is engaged? Let's keep it on the up and up."

In response, Sam stands up, walks over to the wall and puts her leg up into a split against the wall. "Stop being such a rule follower. There is nothing wrong with two attractive people flirting."

Thomas stands up from the ground; he can't tear his eyes away from her. "Listen to your cousin. It's just innocent, eh."

Sam excuses herself to the free weight area and Thomas pounces.

"Why are you blocking my shit, Niko?"

This guy's really is a piece of shit. "You are engaged, right?"

He shrugs. "If you can even call it that. We haven't been intimate once since she got home."

The news hits me right in the center of my heart. I didn't have the right to ask Whitney, but this revelation speaks volumes about the woman that is carving a place in my heart.

"Doesn't mean you can make a play for my cousin."

"Hey, grown woman here." Sam cuts through our conversation. We have played this angle more than once. "If you must know, Niko, Dean and I broke up."

Thomas' smile broadens.

"What? When?" I feign the perfect amount of shock.

"Months ago. It's good. I'm happy."

The set-up is made. I pretend like the shock is too much and I can't watch this unfold. I grab my things and begin to storm out.

"So, you're gonna leave like an angsty teen? You still picking me up for dinner?" Sam shouts after me.

As if on cue, Thomas chimes in and says he would love to escort her.

"Looks like I got dinner covered!" she yells. "But you better get over your shit by tomorrow. I didn't fly across the world to spend time by myself."

I continue to walk away. Hook, line, and sinker.

18

*T*he sun is still high in the sky when Thomas and I arrive at the beach. His idea of dinner is really more of a late lunch, promising that I will be hungry again before bedtime. I'm glad that he has come to his senses and stopped trying to impress me with expensive meals. Al Fresco is a perfect date location. It's really a bunch of food trucks in the parking lot off the beach with picnic tables and paths that lead to beach cabanas. Thomas reserved a cabana for us, and I order a sushi bowl. Thomas orders a poke burrito.

The baby blue summer dress and sandals I'm wearing are perfect for our date. No makeup, and my natural curls blowing in the slight breeze.

Thomas runs back to the food truck to get extra sauce for his burrito and I watch him. His confidence is overwhelming. He's the sort of guy that sits in the coffee shop loudly chatting about the stock market and other business dealings with friends or on his phone. He yearns for everyone around him to know how successful he is before he opens his mouth. I think back to only twenty minutes ago when Thomas picked me up. My dad opened the door to Thomas and you'd have thought a dignitary was entering our home. My parents gushed over Thomas like he was a prize that I should count my lucky stars for daily. If only they knew the real Thomas. It makes me sad watching him now. *Did I ever really know him?*

Thomas makes his way back to our cabana, handing me extra napkins. "I've missed this place so much," I say.

"Yeah, me too. They've done some cool upgrades," Thomas says.

I lean forward and sit cross-legged facing him and start in on my bowl. "Like what?"

He copies the action. "When the sun goes down it's supposed to light up like Christmas," he says, kicking his shoes off.

"That sounds perfect."

Looking around, there are plenty of other couples and small groups of people enjoying a day at the beach. But this is so much more romantic than a usual day. The cabanas are a combination of bed and sofa, allowing plenty of room to stretch out. The rich dark wooden pergola is dressed with thick white sheer material that opens up to the ocean, making the view extraordinary.

"There's music too," he says.

That makes me smile, and as if on cue, soft music floats through the air.

"This place is spectacular, Thomas." I continue to dig into my food. I feel slightly happy; I think things may just be going my way.

"Sorry I haven't been around much; I've been working on some things. Can't have you marrying a pauper," he says, breaking the silence.

I sigh and stare at him for a moment before speaking. "Thomas, when have I ever given you the impression that I care about money? Marriage is for better or for worse. We'll get by, no matter what." I focus on my food and take a couple of bites. When I look up at Thomas, he is staring at me, all smiles.

"I'm so glad you said that, Whit."

We continue eating, finding a comfortable quiet for the first time since he made his business intentions known. My shoulders relax, and the tension leaves my body. This crisis may have been averted.

"Thomas, what do think about London?"

"I love it there," he says around a bite of burrito.

"That's good to hear."

His face bares his curiosity before he says, "Why do you ask?"

I set my food down and inhale a dose of fresh air. Telling your fiancé that you plan to move to another country can be relationship-ending business. "Because I may be relocating there in the fall, and I want you to come with me." I brace myself for his reaction. "We can get the fresh start we both really need." I take another breath and continue. "Maybe you can even go back to school for something else." I wait for his reaction which, at the moment, is a look of confusion, as if I've grown a second head.

Thomas drops his food onto his plate and continues to stare at me but, with each passing second, his expression grows darker. Then, as if a switch inside flips, he smiles—but if his intention is to comfort, he needs a mirror, because it has the opposite effect.

"I thought we discussed this, Whitney. We already have a fresh start. This is happening. You aren't going to London."

"But—" I try to say before he cuts me off.

"We started something here—" He jabs his finger into the sofa. "—and we are going to see it through. Why are you being this way?" I imagine a pot of water set on the stove that is swirling as it builds its way up to boiling when I look at Thomas. He is growing angrier by the second.

A shiver runs through me. I have changed nothing. "I'm not a whore," I mean to say the words with strength and conviction, but my voice fails me, and it comes out small and weak. My heart is hurting once again.

He laughs. "Are you sure about that? Cause if memory serves me, you've already served one customer." He shakes his head at me, smiling like he's already won. Like I flunked a test.

My hand connects with his face before I can stop it. I gasp at my reaction. I have never slapped anyone before. Thomas gapes at me in obvious shock, but he is not nearly as angry as I expected him to be.

"Hmph." He rubs his jaw. "I see." He stiffens. "Now I'm the bad guy, eh, Whitney?"

He stares at me with a look in his eyes that isn't hate, but it's close. "You know, you could have turned me down the other night, walked away, but you didn't. Instead you showed me who you are, no, what you are. You went to the sixth floor and fucked a complete stranger. Which tells me that you'll do anything for me. You're mine."

My palm stings from the contact. My eyes burn with scorching tears. My heart aches from being broken. I try another tactic. Money is what he is hungry for. "I have money saved up, Thomas. You can have it, thirty thousand dollars for your fresh start, our fresh start, in London, away from all of this."

He laughs at me, again. "We've already begun our fresh start, you and me. And in a few months, your thirty thousand will be chump change in comparison. Trust me."

"I'm really trying to, Thomas." I sigh. I feel the sag in my body. When I came to this romantic destination I was full of hope, inflated with the belief that he was past his insane idea, only to sit across from him with my hope deflating like a punctured air mattress. I fear that the longer I sit in front of this man I don't know anymore, the greater the risk that there won't be much left of me.

"You want a refill?" I reach my hand out for his cup, even my arm feels heavy.

"Sure." He hands his cup to me and smirks. "You'll come around to my side. I'm all you got, Whit."

I slip my phone into my pocket, grab my cup and head to the food truck, and mourn my relationship on the way. Tears pierce my eyes. I'm so damned tired of crying. I came home wanting a better life, my old life, but this is worse than The Chamber. At least there I could expect cruelty, to be treated like a whore. The crazy thing is Thomas is treating me worse than anyone at The Chamber ever did.

I make a decision while I wait in the short line and decide to call for a ride.

Me: *Can you come and pick me up? I hate to ask, but I'm breaking up with Thomas, and I don't think it'll be pretty.*

I get an immediate response.

Niko: *Where are you?*

Me: *Al Fresco at the Alcove. Middle cabana.*

Niko: *On my way. Don't break up with him until I get there.*

Me: *K. Thanks.*

Niko: *Erase your text messages to me.*

Great thinking.

I erase our conversation and pull up Instagram while I wait my turn, commenting on pictures from Amaris' photo shoot. When I look up,

Thomas is watching me. When it's my turn, I request the refills, grab our drinks, and head back.

"Here you go," I lean over and hand Thomas his drink.

"Thanks. Who were you talking to?"

I give him a look of confusion. "I was checking on things, mainly Amaris' latest photo shoot." I pull out my phone and pull up her Instagram pics and show him, pretending that the photo shoot is the most exciting thing I've seen in a long time.

He glances at her photos in a noncommittal way. "Can I see your ring?" he asks when I take a seat. I reach my arm out to show him my ring. "Not like that, take it off and show it to me."

I do as he requests and hand him the ring, watching as he slips it into his pocket.

"What're you doing with that?" I ask.

He leans back against the fluffy pillows. "You'll get it back."

"When?" I act concerned. Even if this is the last time I plan to ever see him, I'm still curious about his intentions.

He stares at me. "When you come to your senses and realize that this is the deal me made. And you *will* come around, because *I'm* all you have," he repeats himself. He has made it his point to remind me every chance he gets. But what he doesn't know is that it couldn't be further from the truth.

Would I stay if he was all that I had, if I didn't have a stronger shoulder to cry on? If there wasn't another competitor waiting in the wings? I know the answer to that question without giving it a second thought.

I am weak.

But to save myself from what Thomas has planned for me I will grab onto any lifeline I can. For me, right now, that happens be Niko Andres—my knight, my shoulder, my friend.

As if he rode in on an actual white horse, wearing a white hat, Niko appears.

"Hey, guys," he says in his smooth voice that already has too comforting an effect on me. I can feel the tension melt away because I know I am in good hands now.

Thomas hops up from the cabana and reaches out his hand in greeting, as if Niko just happened to show up, passing by on his way to stroll the beach or dine at Al Fresco. Thomas greets him as if this is a total coincidence. "Niko, what are you doing here? You could have called me if you wanted to hire us for another special night. We are definitely open for business."

Niko doesn't accept his offered hand. He looks down at it and back up into Thomas' eyes with a glare.

"I came to pick up Whitney," he says.

Thomas looks completely taken off guard. When I walk over and stand beside Niko, his confusion gives way to anger.

"What the hell are you talking about? Whitney isn't going anywhere with you." A muscle in his jaw contracts, and I gaze down and see his hands fisting and relaxing. "Whitney isn't going anywhere with you," he repeats through gritted teeth.

My heart is pounding in my chest. "I called Niko to come and pick me up. It's over, Thomas." I take a step closer to Niko.

Thomas stares between the two of us. He isn't a big man, but he is strong. I watch as Thomas sizes Niko up, deciding if he can take him. I can see the moment when he realizes the odds are stacked against him.

"This isn't over, Whitney. You work for me. You think you can call your first customer to save you? No, I see, the two of you plan to go into business together." He glares at Niko. "You think she'll be your whore, instead of mine, eh? Ain't gonna happen."

My feet are frozen in the sand, and my legs feel like lead pipes. This is what I'm reduced to in Thomas' eyes. It was never going to work between us because he holds me accountable for what happened to me. I should have seen the truth the day I came home. His questions were less about how I was doing, if I was okay, and more about why I stayed so long, why I never tried to leave, wondering just how much I fought—as if I chose to be there. His business wheels set to spinning at that moment. *If she can stay for her captor, what would she do for the man she loves?* He is an animal. I hate him with every fiber of my being.

Niko moves. He steps toward Thomas, directly into his space. "Say another contrary word about Whitney and I will beat you senseless, you piece of shit."

"She is my fiancé. She stays with me." Thomas doesn't back down; he puffs his chest out and tries to take advantage of every inch of his available height, but his voice lacks the initial confidence.

"You don't get it, do you? You had your chance, and you fucked it up. Whitney is a beautiful woman who spent a year in hell, and when she gets back you think it's a fine idea to pimp her out?"

Thomas' eyes cut to me and his stare is menacing. I never thought he would be capable of hurting me physically, but the way he is looking at me I now know he is capable of anything.

Thomas speaks up, his eyes never leave mine. "Whitney is a smart girl. She knows this is about business, and she knows I love her. You have to know that I love you."

I look down at the ground. "Doesn't matter." I pause for a moment to control my breathing. "I'm not what you want me to be, and I never will be. I keep trying to make you forget this idea and you won't. So, it's over, Thomas."

He starts laughing. His whole body shakes. Niko takes a step back, landing in a protective stance, ready to strike. Thomas bends over and continues laughing at something humorous that we have not been privy to. "I'm sorry. But this is some funny shit." He pauses and glances back between the two of us. Pointing his finger at us.

"You fucked this guy—a perfect stranger—for me. And now you're breaking up with me to be with the guy you fucked?" He stops talking to laugh some more. He holds up a finger, sucks in some air, and says, "But wait, let's not forget to add you got paid to sleep with him. Correction. I got paid." He stops laughing and takes a few more breaths. Tears from laughing so hard fill his eyes. "Get your ass over here next to me, Whitney. You are a whore and you're mine." He says, no longer laughing. He stares daggers at me, and deep down inside I believe he thinks I will step away from Niko and join. "I'm waiting."

Niko leans forward, a huge grin on his face. "You think you're a comedian, huh?"

Thomas smiles and nods.

"Jokes on you, asshole. We—" Niko gestures between him and I. "Never had sex." He quiets and waits for his words to sink in. Niko leaks and oozes confidence. I soak some of it up and stand a little taller. I can't wait to see this all go down. The moment when Thomas realizes that he has lost me for good, that he can't control me, that I don't belong to him—the moment that the smug look is wiped off of his face permanently.

"Bullshit," Thomas says finally.

It's Niko's turn to laugh. "Come on, Thomas, let's all have a seat and I'll tell you a sweet little story."

Thomas hesitates and looks around.

"Stop. We're all friends here. Let's sit. You'll love this story."

Thomas and Niko take a seat. I don't. I can't, my nerves are pulled wire tight. I stand in front of them though, nearest to Niko. I wouldn't miss this show.

"So, I meet this guy about seven months ago. Seems like a nice enough fellow. I can tell right away that he has shrewd business skills, but has fallen on some bad luck. In all our meetings he never mentions his missing girlfriend. So, this guy and I meet a few times for beers. I like him. We start training together, and I don't even charge him. I even feel sorry for him because there was something sad behind his eyes. So, imagine my surprise when my new friend approaches me months later and tells me that he has an idea for a new business and needs to start with some customers that he can trust."

Thomas is seething already.

"It's not my thing, paying for sex. But I consider this guy a friend, and I help my friends." Niko scoots closer to Thomas and drapes his arm around shoulders. "I sit upstairs in a hotel room on the sixth floor with twenty-five hundred dollars in my pocket. My heart is racing. The whole thing is highly illegal. But I told myself, I'd help out this one time. I didn't have to wait long before the door opens and the most beautiful woman walks through. She doesn't look like a pro. No, she looks scared to death. It's obvious by her red eyes that she'd been crying. I mean this poor woman is so afraid that I can *see* her body shaking. Can you imagine someone shaking so hard that you can see it with your own eyes? I want you to take a moment and imagine this."

"Listen—" Thomas tries to move and interrupt, but Niko tightens his hold around Thomas, and I can see him wince in pain.

"No, no, the story isn't over. You have to hear it in its entirety to fully understand." Niko says, pulling Thomas closer to him. Thomas tries to wiggle away, but Niko is too strong. "Don't get antsy now, I'm almost to the good part." Niko laughs a little. I'm about to jump out of my skin. I was there, but it is insane hearing the story of how we met from his point of view.

Niko continues. "I offer the beautiful lady a seat. Thomas, I could see her chest rising and falling. She was so afraid. I decide to talk to her. Ease her fears. Do you know what I learn about her?"

Thomas doesn't say anything.

"I'll ask again. Do you know what I learned about her?"

"No, what?" Thomas asks between tight lips.

"She told me that she was kidnapped and made to have sex with strangers for an entire year before she was released. She also told me that she was only released about three weeks before that night. I don't even know her and I felt protective of her, any respectable man would."

Niko takes his time, letting this all sink in. He looks off into the ocean, lost in the moment. I see it in his face—the hurt, the anger. "But the worst part of everything she told me, worse than hearing how she suffered, was learning that the man downstairs who sent her up to spend the night with me was her fiancé." He lets his words hang in the air.

"I wanted to do two things. Run down the stairs and beat the shit out of my friend. I mean, really break him." He balls up his fist and squeezes it. "I wanted to break so many bones that the piece of shit downstairs remembered what a deplorable human being he was during all of the months of his healing. He looks up at me; a sweet smile crosses his face. "Then, I wanted to take this beautiful woman into my arms and protect her, heal her." I return the endearment, a thrill shoots through me at his words, it feels warm. The smile goes away when he turns his attention back to Thomas.

"So, Thomas, what do you think happened?"

He shrugs.

"I'll tell you what happened. The beautiful lady offers me a counter. She offers to pay me double to not sleep with her and keep it from you."

Thomas looks up at me and interrupts, "You lied to me?"

I don't answer. I look down. The anger behind his eyes shoots through me, and even though I know I'm safe right now, the heat behind his eyes makes me shiver.

"Uh, uh. This is my story." Niko laughs. "Me being the gentleman that I am, I took her counter. She wired me five thousand dollars."

He turns to me. "Remind me to give that money back to you," he says. "Or, maybe we can use it to take a vacation. You mentioned on the phone last night that you want to travel," he says, and I know he's provoking Thomas. He gets what he wants as Thomas' face frowns into a grimace at the mention of our phone conversation.

"We talked for a couple of hours in that room. I told her she needed to get away from you. What we did not do upstairs, on the sixth floor, was have sex. I didn't even touch her. Right, Whitney?"

I stare at Thomas and respond, "Right." My words come out shaky.

"Surprise. So, you see, you and Whitney are in fact over. You had the chance to treat her right and you fucked that up. So, today, you get to say goodbye. I want you to look at her."

I know Thomas is looking at me, I can feel my skin crawl. Even though I don't want to lock onto his gaze, I know I have to. So I do. Thomas is fuming.

"Thomas. She isn't mine, but she sure as fuck isn't yours. You are no longer my friend; she is. This is a warning from a former friend. Stay the fuck away from her. Now please, say goodbye." He squeezes him again, and Thomas winces audibly.

"Goodbye, Whitney." It comes out in a grunt.

"Goodbye," I say.

Niko stands up and returns to my side. "Now, wasn't that a great story full of surprises?" Niko says with a smile. I expect him to laugh, but he doesn't. Instead he takes my hand and we walk away.

19

WHITNEY

*B*y the time I get into Niko's truck, I'm shaking. Niko opens the door, and I climb inside with a little help from him. I shouldn't look back at Thomas, but I can't resist the urge. He's standing up watching us. My heart stutters when he waves at me. Something tells me that his goodbye was too easy.

I jump when Niko closes his door.

"Are you okay?" he asks.

I shake my head. "But, I will be. Thank you for everything."

"Are you kidding? It was my pleasure." He puts the truck in reverse and backs out.

I sink into the seat and relax, letting the sense of safety envelop me. The silence feels good. A weight is lifted now that Thomas knows I didn't sleep with Niko. Hallelujah. Even though we're not together, I couldn't have him thinking I would become a prostitute.

"Where to?" he asks.

"Anyplace but here."

"You want me to take you home?"

"Not home. They think I'm on a date with Thomas. If I come home early, they'll wonder what's wrong. Besides, I didn't get to finish eating, I'm starved."

"I know just the place," Niko says. "But, you know you have to tell your family about Thomas."

I turn my head and look at him. Niko is gorgeous. I take advantage of his need to watch the road and I stare. The muscles in his arms don't even need to flex to show the definition as he holds the steering wheel, and now, I want nothing more than to be inside of those strong arms.

"Did you get a haircut?" I ask, changing the subject. His brown hair is shorter than the last time I saw him, but it's still styled in the messy just woke up look.

"Yes, I did, you like?" he smiles.

"I do." I blush. I take a couple of breaths before I begin. "Look, I know I have to tell my folks. It's just...they are finally getting to a place where they are letting their guard down where I'm concerned. You're the only one who knows the truth about what a mess I really am."

He laughs.

"Why are you laughing at me?" I ask with a nervous laugh.

"Trust me, I'm not laughing at you, exactly. I mean, I am because you're so cute sometimes. I don't think you're a mess. You, my friend, have to give yourself some credit; you've been through a lot, and your handling it very well."

I look out the window. I wish I could see myself the way he sees me. He said the friend word again. "Yeah, yeah, I know."

After driving a short distance we pull into an unfamiliar building.

"Where are we?" I ask.

"Just a place that'll work you up into a real hunger and if you're up for it, we'll go to dinner," he says. "Okay?"

I nod and smile.

Butterflies attack my stomach when he smiles back at me. Niko makes his way to my side of the car. Normally, I get out of the car on my own. I don't mind a man opening my door when I am getting into the car, but waiting for a man to open my door feels weird. But, Niko's car is a million miles off the ground; I actually need assistance getting out.

Instead of holding my hand and assisting me, he picks me up, like I weigh nothing, and sets me down. His hands are so big and strong, how can I not feel safe? When he lets go, I feel the absence. If it were right, I would put his hands back on me.

"You ready?" he asks.

"Curious. Not sure about ready."

He laughs and then puts an arm around me, guiding me through the door. When we walk inside, I immediately regret giving him carte blanche on where to take me. *A boxing gym? Why?* The place is modern and sleek with several boxing rings scattered about, mats and standalone punching bags. I follow Niko to a counter. An older gentleman with ebony-toned skin is sitting on a chair behind the counter. His eyes light with excitement at seeing us approach.

"Look what the cat dragged in," he says and stands from his chair. He looks to be in his seventies, but he moves like a much younger man. He comes from behind the counter. "Niko, it is good to see you." They hug like old friends. The man only comes to Niko's chest level.

"Milo, it's good to see you, too."

They break from the hug and Milo turns to me. "You brought a beautiful young lady," he says.

"Milo, this is my friend, Whitney. I brought her here to work out."

I extend my hand to Milo's and he takes it, bringing it to his lips. "You are in capable hands, Ms. Whitney. If you need anything, I'm your man," he says and smiles.

"Thank you," I say, glowing inside and out.

I turn to Niko and look at him as though he's lost his mind.

"You do realize I'm in a dress and sandals. Not exactly boxing attire." I point to myself.

He laughs at me. "We're not here to spar, just play. Next time I will give you a heads up when I bring you here."

Next time. I smile.

Niko and I head into the gym, and it's clear to me that he knows just about everyone. He gives high fives, fist bumps, and hugs to guys of all ages. We stop in front of two young adorable boys, no older than six. Niko holds his hands up, and the boys take turns punching; he pretends that it hurts him. When he's done, he pats the kids in a way that is paternal and my heart swells. *Who is this guy?*

I follow him to a quiet area in the back to a mat and a row of heavy bags. I place my small handbag on the mat and stand with him. "This area back here is used for personal trainers. Come here, closer."

I make the few steps toward him and wind up standing in front of the bag.

"Do you know how to make a fist?"

"Of course." I shake my head at him and ball my hand into a fist.

Niko takes my hand into his. It looks like the hand of a child. He studies my fist. "Not bad, Whittie," he says. He walks to a small closet and produces a pair of boxing gloves. He helps me into the gloves. I look up at him the entire time. Into his intense blue eyes. He is the only one who sees me—not my family, not my friends, certainly not my ex, only this man. He smiles down at me, his lips soft and full. I would never be bold enough to kiss him.

"Make a fist just like you showed me and punch the bag," he says after he helps me into the gloves.

I turn away from him and toward the bag. I pull back my fist and hit it. I probably look insane wearing boxing gloves, punching a heavy bag in a dress and sandals.

"Again," he says. This time when I punch the bag he makes minor adjustments to my stance and how I'm holding my arms. "Non-punching arm goes here." He places my arm near the side of my head. "This way you can protect your sweet face if someone were to swing at you." Even as he says it, I can see that the idea of someone hitting me is unsettling to him. "How does it feel?" Niko moves behind the bag and gestures for me to keep punching it.

"This feels amazing, like nothing I've ever done before." I hit the bag over and over; the bag might as well have Thomas' face plastered on it, because that's who I'm pretending to hit.

"Small but mighty," Niko laughs. "You're a natural."

Niko walks away from the bag. I'm feeling sweaty from exertion. I wish I'd have known I'd feel like this, I would have pulled my hair up. *Next time.* The thought makes me smile.

"What are you smiling about?" Niko asks.

When he appears from behind my bag he is shirtless. And let me just say, Niko shirtless is like looking at a fitness model. I can't help myself; I freeze mid-punch and gape at him, which makes him laugh harder. He's built like he never misses a workout, lean in the waist with that V that doesn't disappoint. He waves a gloved hand in front of me.

"Whittie, are you okay?"

I snap out of my daze. They say it's rude to stare, but if he didn't want me to he would have kept his shirt on. I'm sure if I stripped out of my dress he'd have a similar reaction. I punch him in his thirty-pack of abs. "Stop calling me that stupid nickname," I say, but I smile, which means he'll never stop. I gesture at his gorgeous body. "Just friends or not, you're gonna have to put your shirt back on."

He laughs and starts hitting the bag. "It's just a body, Whit...ney."

I shake my head fast, trying to extinguish my desires. "Uh, no, it's not."

We stand side-by-side beating up our bags. I stop looking at his body and focus on releasing the remaining tension from my body. When we're done, I am drenched. My hair has lost most of its curls and the second the gloves are off, I gather it up and twirl it into a bun on top of my head. Niko tosses me a towel and I dry off. I follow him to take a seat on a bench and down the water he hands me.

"When can we do this again?" I ask, looking at him. He still doesn't have his shirt on, and the towel draped around him is even sexier.

"You liked it?" he asks, his eyebrows raise in surprise.

"I loved it. I could release so much into that bag."

He drinks his water and doesn't wipe it off when some of it rolls down his throat. I have to look away because my mind is thinking about how much I want to lick it off.

"Good, because your training has officially started." He finishes the water and successfully hits the trash can, throwing it like a basketball into a hoop.

I turn my attention from the trash and back to him. "Training?"

He hoists his leg over the bench so that he's facing me. He's so close that I can feel the heat from his body. "I told you when we first met that you made me worry about you. I don't trust Thomas. I'd feel a lot better if I knew you could protect yourself, so I plan to teach you how. Is that okay? You're important to me."

I look down. I'm embarrassed. "Are you this protective of all your friends?" I ask.

"Another thing I told you, I want to be more." His voice is heavy and low.

When I look up, he's moved closer. If I move half an inch we'd be touching. So, I do it. I move, and his lips are warm and sweet. Our kiss is slow and sexy. I inhale him, the mixture of the lavender and mint I've already come to associate with comfort and safety makes my head light, and the butterflies go to war inside of me. He breaks the kiss way too soon, but not the eye contact.

"Was that okay? I don't want to rush with you."

"It was breathtaking." I blush. I could stay under his gaze for an eternity.

He smiles shyly.

After a long silence, we both rise from the bench and head for the front of the gym. Niko takes me by the hand. "Come on, let me get some food in you."

"I look a mess, I can't go out like this." I stop in my tracks.

Niko turns around and walks back to me, even his gait is sexy. This time when he kisses me it is quick and sweet, leaving me wanting more. "You look beautiful."

This makes me smile, but no amount of flattery will be enough for me to go out like this. "I think I'd rather you just take me home. I have a date with a tuna sandwich. If you want to hang out at my place, I make a mean one," I say before I can stop myself. This is all wrong. I shouldn't be kissing him or letting him kiss me. I certainly shouldn't be inviting him back to my house. The lines are so blurry, I can't see straight. Thomas and I literally broke up less than two hours ago. I mean, the sun is still out, and I'm already kissing another man. Getting close to Niko is a mistake, and I know why. I fight the thoughts flooding my brain. *If he wasn't here, where would you be right now?* The answer is, I truly don't know. *He made it easy to say goodbye to Thomas, but if he wasn't there would I have stayed? Would I have done the things he asked of me? And if so, what does that say about me? How much strength did leaving Thomas behind really take on my part if I had a knight ready to save me?*

I have to tread lightly with Niko because the more I depend on him, the less I can depend on me. I definitely can't let him kiss me again, no matter how bad I might want him to.

Niko nudges me out of my thoughts. "That sounds like an offer I can't refuse."

20

On the way to my house, I realize the huge mistake I've made. I was so excited to spend more time with Niko that I didn't realize the implications of bringing him home with me. I don't live alone, I live with my parents. The downside of being a prodigy, my mental abilities were always leaps and bounds beyond the skills that I need to take care of myself—making me often appear much younger than I am. I was on the fast track to catching up before I was taken, and being in The Chamber made me grow up even faster. My parents won't see it that way. Time is a sneaky bandit. My parents and I experienced the year I was gone in very different ways. The Chamber made me stronger, a survivor. Whilst it also made me weaker, unsure of my own worth. For my family, my time away made them want to hold on tighter, entrusting almost no one with my safety—they too were snowed by Thomas' sociopathic charms. He conned his way into everyone's hearts.

No one is in the front room when we walk inside. I know my parents are home. They're always home, or close to it. I want to change clothes quickly, but I have to make sure my family knows there is a strange man sitting in the kitchen—a strange man with skin the color of cream.

I knock on my parent's door. "Hey, I'm back. I wanted to let you know I brought a friend home." I say through the door, waiting for a response. The door swings open, and I am face-to-face with my father. "Hi, Daddy. He's a male friend." I stumble over my words. The way Daddy is looking at me, I know I need to add more information. "Actually, he's more my trainer. Can you come meet him really quick?" I can see the skepticism in my father's eyes, but he calls for my mom and they both follow me to the kitchen.

Niko stands when we walk into the kitchen. "Mr. and Mrs. Alexander, it is so nice to meet you. My name is Nikolai Andres, but my friends call me Niko." He extends his hand out to Daddy.

They shake hands, but I can see from the twitch in Daddy's jaw that he isn't happy that Niko is standing in their kitchen. "Nice to meet you," my parents say. They take a seat at the table, and Niko and I follow. I'm so sweaty, and all I want to do is change clothes, but this is my mistake. I was so excited about any extra time I could get with Niko that I sped head-first into introductions with my folks. And of course, Niko being ever confident, didn't hesitate. Daddy begins his line of questioning.

"So how do you know my daughter again?"

Niko clears his throat. "We met through a mutual acquaintance. Thomas."

My parents both relax and smiles cross their faces. It stuns me to really see the pedestal they have Thomas placed on. "You're friends with her fiancé," my mother says as relief floods her face. For simple beach folk, they sure seem all about appearances.

"Friends is a stretch." Niko does an amazing job of keeping his voice light, not revealing his disdain for Thomas through his words. "We run in the same circle. I'm a trainer down at Milo's."

My father's eyebrows raise, and he smiles. "I haven't been there in a few years. How is ol' Milo?"

A warm smile warms Niko's face. "Milo is well, still moves like a young man and swears he can take all of us in a three rounder."

Niko and my dad laugh. "Don't underestimate him," Dad says.

"I never do." His hands raise in mock defeat. And I think back to the sweet tiny man that greeted us at the front desk.

Dad sits back in his chair. The familiarity of Milo's relaxes him where Niko is concerned.

"So, what kind of training are you giving our daughter?" my mother asks.

I chime in. "Boxing, self-defense. After what happened, I thought it might be a good idea. It's exhausting but necessary."

My parents exchange glances. "And, Thomas is okay with this training?" Daddy asks. "I'm sure there are female trainers down at Milo's," he adds.

The sigh escapes me before I can stop it. My parents aren't fooling anyone with their smiles. They are not happy with Niko being here for one second. I know it, and they know I know it. But, they are being polite. "I am a grown person. So that means I don't belong to Thomas, or anyone. I am free to choose who to train with." What I don't say is that Thomas and I broke up. There's plenty of time for me to tell them the news, preferably not in the presence of someone they just met.

"Guys, can you keep Niko company? I'm gonna go change. We're going for a run on the beach. Conditioning," I say and roll my eyes implying that the activity is the last thing I want to do, when in reality, I need to get Niko out of here. "Be right back," I say to Niko with a look loaded with apologies for leaving him alone with my folks.

I run back to my room in a panic. My parents are nosey with their sweet smiles and island hospitality. I grab a damp towel and wipe my face, thankful that I wasn't wearing any makeup. I redo my bun, towel dry, reapply deodorant, and throw on workout clothes and sneakers. I jog into the kitchen and sure enough, they are giving him the full-blown how many questions can we squeeze in before Whitney returns. I'm not angry with them for this. If my daughter was kidnapped, I'd question any stranger that she is newly acquainted with, especially one of Niko's formidable size. But, I know some of their questions are more about their misplaced allegiance to Thomas.

"Let's go," I say.

They all rise. "How long will you be gone?" Daddy asks.

I roll my eyes before I can stop myself. "Daddy," I whine and let out a breath. I have to remember my family suffered my kidnapping too. "We're going running right down the street at the beach. We'll probably grab food and walk back. If you get worried, call me, or come workout with us," I offer, but only because I know my dad's theory about running. He always says, *if you see me running, you better start running too, cause something bad is coming.*

"I'll pass on that, but keep your phone on." Daddy takes an authoritative stance, and he is nearly as big as Niko. He shakes Niko's hand. "There's a lot of evil in this world, Niko. Remember that when you're training my baby."

Niko smiles. "Yes, sir." He turns and shakes my mother's hand, and we head out the door.

"That was intense," Niko says when we hit the sidewalk. We don't run, we walk. In fact, if Niko broke out into a run I would throw something at him. I am dying of hunger and a story about us training was my only way to get us out of the house. I have no plans of getting my heart rate above a medium tempo.

"Sorry about that. Sometimes I forget that I don't live alone. They mean well."

Niko smirks. "They love you."

All I can do is smile because he's right about that. We walk in silence until we reach the beach and stop at the first burger place we find. "I'm so hungry right now, I think my body might be eating itself." I bend forward and hold my grumbling belly.

"You are theatrical, aren't you?"

I smack his arm playfully. "Did you just call me a drama queen?"

"Absolutely not," he replies in a sarcastic tone.

He orders from the menu. The only thing they serve is burgers and fries, that's it. But their food is known on the island.

"Two burgers, two fries—" Niko says.

"Oh, and a vanilla shake," I add to the order.

"A vanilla shake and a chocolate shake." Niko smiles, and I shake my head. I can feel my cheeks warm. His flirting takes my mind off my hunger long enough for the food to arrive.

We find a seat at a table; the sun is going down, and the view is spectacular.

"So, what are you going to say to your folks?"

I plant my face into my hands, before I say, "I don't know."

He laughs at me and says, "The truth works really well. I'd start with that."

"You're teasing me. You have no idea the pedestal my mom and dad have Thomas on."

He takes a monster bite of his burger. "Sounds like it's time for him to be knocked off that pedestal."

I know that he's right. But to do that means that I have to admit the awful person that he has become, which is a fine way to knock him down, but to admit that is monumentally embarrassing for me. How do you tell your parents the man you thought you loved, the man they adore, wanted to turn you into a prostitute? My dad will probably kill him.

We eat in silence, and my belly is grateful for every bite. Every few minutes, I take a glance at Niko and find him smiling at me.

"I'm moving to London," I blurt out.

Niko's face bares his surprise before he can cover it. "Is that so?"

I nod. "Well, I think so. I emailed the school in London that I should be at right now. I'm waiting to see if they will agree to take me back."

Niko smiles at me. "That sounds amazing. I love London; I'm sure they'll take you back. When would you start?"

I chew a bite of my burger. "Not until the fall, so we have plenty of time to train. I mean, if you still want to do that." I look down.

"That's plenty of time to get you ready," he says. I stare into his blue eyes. He really is a beautiful man.

He reaches across the small table and swipes his finger on the side of my mouth. "You had a little mustard," he says and wipes his fingers on his napkin. The touch does something to me inside. Butterflies thrash around my abdomen, giving me goosebumps, and I know I'm blushing.

"What exactly will I be ready for?" I ask, not taking my eyes from his.

"Anything."

Oh, good lord. This man makes my head dizzy. If he leaned forward and kissed me, I don't think I would stop him, even though I know I should.

"I'd better get you home. Your dad seems like the type of man whose good side I need to stay on."

I laugh at that thought. We begin the walk back and talk about training. My reaction to Niko slipping his hand into mine, surprises me. I do nothing. I allow it. I crave it in the deepest parts of my being, and it is more natural than I could have ever guessed it could be.

Hand in hand, we deliberately take slow steps back to the house.

He discusses with me the plans he has to take me through all the paces—strengthening, conditioning, boxing, defensive techniques, including weapons. When Niko is done with me, I will be far more difficult to kidnap.

"Are you sure you don't want me to pay you?" I ask when we are halfway to my house.

Niko stops and turns to me. His blue eyes are like staring into a deep ocean. "I will consider myself paid in full when you can defend yourself enough that I don't have to worry about you so much."

I blush. "You act like you're sitting at home worrying for my safety on the daily." I look down at our feet, both in sneakers without running a step.

"Something like that," he says, making my head snap up and look at him.

My head swims in the moment. The sun kisses my skin, the sky is dark blue and cloudless, the sea air cools me with its intermittent breeze, and I'm standing hand in hand with this man who stares at me like I am something special, someone to be protected and worried about. He asks me for nothing in return.

"Then I'm just gonna have to work harder. I don't want worry lines to mar that beautiful face of yours."

Niko laughs lightly at my compliment. We turn and continue our walk to my house. If I could be honest with him and myself, I'd walk past the house and make my time with him last. But this will have to do for now.

When we arrive at my front door, neither of us makes a move. When the silence is too much, and we play bashful and shy with one another long enough, Niko kisses me on the cheek and walks away. I watch him climb into his truck and then I walk into my house.

21

WHITNEY

"*H*ave you lost your damn mind bringing a stranger into our home? Daddy's voice booms at me before I close the door.

I roll my eyes at him. "Calm down, Daddy. He isn't a stranger to me, and I told you we are just friends." I lean against the door. My father is all about how things look to other people, so I can't leave in the middle of whatever this is, but I really want to.

"It isn't proper, Whitney." He points to the couch, and I take a seat where he's pointing.

"Because he's white? I didn't figure you for a racist." I stare at him.

"What do I care if the boy is white? Hell, my grandmother is white and you know that. He could be purple for all I care. What I do care about is you disgracing yourself." He takes a couple of breaths. "An engaged woman shouldn't be spending time alone with a single man."

He's huffing mad.

"I spoke to Milo and he said you and this Niko character were awfully chummy at the gym. He said if he didn't know you were with Thomas, he'd have thought you were with this fellow."

What? It's my turn to be angry.

"So, you're checking up on me now, Daddy? How dare you?"

I stand up from the couch just as Mom comes into the living room. I'm done with all of this.

No, done isn't a strong enough word. I'm exhausted. "You know what? Maybe I don't want to be engaged. Thomas and I broke up earlier today." I just put it out there, dropping the news like a bomb. Why keep pretending? They don't have to know the why's, not right now—maybe not ever. They need to know it's over, and if they keep after me about how amazing Thomas is, I'll leave.

It takes everything I have to look up at my parents and their faces are a mask of disappointment. *How could I be so stupid?* Is written all over Daddy's face.

"I can't believe what I'm hearing. Did you leave your good sense at that place you were taken to?" Daddy asks.

His words burn me.

I gasp audibly and so does my mother.

Daddy is never mean to me—protective, but never mean. I want so badly to tell him what a monster Thomas has become, perhaps has always been. But the admission is shameful on a cellular level. What if my parents see me that way too? Like I wanted to do those things, like I wanted to stay. I know people want to ask, I can see it in their eyes.

Why did you stay, Whit?

Why did you come out of there looking so pampered?

Where are the bruises? Shouldn't you have bruises?

If only people could understand that not all abuse and suffering is visible.

I smirk. The sound that escapes my lips is sarcastic and disrespectful to my folks. I take a cue from Niko, he is the best smirker.

"Wow, whatever, guys," I say, so mad I can't begin to get into a lengthy conversation. I'm crying before I make it to my room. I think my dad may have hurt me just as much as Thomas.

I check my email. Nothing from London. Hell, maybe I should just move there now. I can go to the admissions office in person. There is nothing for me here. In London, I can get a fresh start without the looks. A plan starts forming in my head. Then I remember my training; I remember Niko. Suddenly training with him becomes important. If I can protect myself against some of the evil in the world, wouldn't I be a more confident person?

My phone rings. It's Chalice. "Hey, girl," I say into the phone.

"Hey, you good?" she asks, and I can hear it in her voice. Mom called in reinforcements.

"My mom called you?" I roll my eyes, an action that is now more common on my face than tears streaming.

Before she can answer, I get a text from Amaris.

Amaris: *Girl, your mom just texted me and said you and Thomas broke up? What's going on? You okay?*

We did, and I'm fine. I reply.

"You wanna go grab a drink and talk?" Chalice asks.

"Not tonight," I say. "Maybe we can head to the shops this weekend. Some retail therapy sounds good."

"Perfect. Call me if you need anything," she says, and we hang up.

This is so exhausting. I wonder how my chamber sisters are holding up. The last time I spoke to anyone of them it was with Flame, I mean Vivian. When we spoke, things were better with Thomas. Things were good. But then I'd only been home about a week. So much has changed. My bones ache and a heaviness engulfs my body. With what little energy I have I climb onto my bed, grab my pillow and pull it into my chest and weep softly.

I WAKE to a knock on my door. It's now dark outside.

"Come in," I say, thinking it's probably Chalis. I wouldn't be surprised if my mother and father don't have the entire island come to see if I'm okay, and check in to make sure that I haven't actually lost my mind.

"Your dad called me," Thomas says and crosses into my room.

I shoot up in my bed. My instinct to scream is strong. "What in the actual fuck are you doing here, Thomas?"

He takes cautious steps toward me. "I told you, Whit. Your folks called me."

My body tenses as he nears. I pop up from my bed and open the distance he is trying to close, but my room isn't that big. "I want you to leave, Thomas. Now."

Who the hell does he think he is? He really didn't get the message earlier today that it was over? I put my hands up and he stops in his tracks.

"Don't be this way, baby. I fucked up. I get it now. I'm sorry. Don't I deserve a second chance?"

He is so full of shit that I nearly erupt in laughter. Thomas is nuts if he thinks he deserves anything from me. I pick up my cell phone and press the number for home. I can hear the phone ringing throughout my house. Daddy's voice breaks through my phone.

"Can you please come to my room?" I say and hang up.

Both Daddy and Mom open my door and walk in, making the tight space seem even smaller.

"What's the problem?" Daddy asks. His big hopeful smile on his face angers me.

I cross my arms over my chest. "This is wrong. I told you we broke up. But, instead of asking why, you decide to invite the man I broke up with into my room. You have to check with me first. I have all the rights here. Especially after everything I went through. If you love this piece of shit so much, you guys marry him!" I yell at my folks.

"Whitney, watch your mouth. Thomas is a fine young man. He is respected within our community. You would do well to marry someone like him," Mom says.

When I glance over at Thomas he is beaming. He knows me well enough to know that I won't mention his business idea. "Whatever. I'm going to sleep in Willa's room. And, since you can't respect my wishes, I'll be looking for my own place tomorrow." I push passed all of them, leaving them stunned by my outburst, and I seriously don't care. The dam breaks by the time I get to my sister's room. I flop onto her bed and cry. I don't wish I was back at The Chamber, but I certainly don't want to be here anymore. If I can't couch surf at one of my sisters' houses, then I can check into a hotel until I can get to London.

This is not the life I expected to come back to. I've been home for nearly two months and everything is shit. When I was locked up at The Chamber, I shared so many Thomas stories with the other girls. I spoke of my beautiful little island town and my parents with such affection.

But now, I see they care more about what is proper than what is right for me. I know that I haven't told them the entire story, but they should trust me enough to make my own decisions and support me.

My father believes that I should be someone's wife. Hell, if I told them the truth about Thomas they'd probably think I was making the whole thing up. They believe Thomas is a prize and never asked me why we broke up. They don't think I can do any better than him, I know it. I desperately want to call Niko; he'd know how to comfort me, but I can't. I'll never know how to comfort myself if I keep letting him do it.

22

WHITNEY

"*I* wish we would have thought of this sooner," Chalice says as she helps me with the few boxes I brought to her cottage.

"Are you sure it's okay? I hate making you lose your media room."

She waves my comment away. "Sweets, please. This is hardly a media room. Besides, Amaris is never home and I hate living alone. This will be perfect, us rooming together."

She blasts music in the darling, three-bedroom cottage. The feeling is light as we dance and unpack my new room. Most likely, I'll only be here a couple more months before heading to London. But I'd rather do the time here with Chalice.

Three hours later and we are sitting on the sofa drinking wine.

"So, was it that bad the other day with your folks that you have to slum it with me?"

I look around. "This place is adorable and hardly slumming." I put my feet up on the table and take a couple healthy sips of wine. "It was time I got some space from them. I know they mean well."

She turns on the television. "Well their loss is my gain. We should Facetime with Amaris. I haven't told her yet," she says and dials Amaris' number.

"What's up, ya'll?" Amaris' face pops onto the screen.

"We got a new roommate, when are you coming home?"

"Ahh. Seriously? It's about time!" Amaris yells. "In that case, I will be heading back early next week. We have to celebrate."

"Sounds like that'll be just in time for a new roomie party," I say.

"Sounds like a date. We'll have everything ready when you get here."

Amaris flashes the peace sign. "I gotta run. See you gals next week." She disconnects the call.

I have no idea why I didn't think of moving in with Chalice in the first place. The mood is light over here. If she does have questions, she's the type to ask them, rather than stare at me in wonder.

"Chick flick?" she asks.

"Yes, ma'am."

I run into the kitchen and grab the wine bottle and chips and dip we got from the store earlier. When I get back to the living room, Chalice already has a blanket out for us.

"I got the snacks. Let the sappy love story marathon commence," I say and plop everything on the table and crawl into the blanket. Chalice picked a funny rom-com for the first movie.

The wine is kicking in and a nice buzz warms my body. My phone pings an alert.

Niko: *Hey stranger. I haven't heard from you all day. Are you okay? We still on for training tomorrow?*

Me: *Of course, we're still on. I've been busy. I moved out of the house, and I'm staying at Chalice's. You remember meeting her?*

Niko: *I do. I guess I missed you. And needed to check on you.*

"Hey. Who are you texting?" Chalice says and snatches my phone from my hand.

"Chalice! Give me my phone back." I shout and run after her, because in true Chalice form she gets up and runs with it, locking herself in the bathroom. "Are you serious? Come out right now!"

The door opens. Her expression is serious. She hands me my phone. I glance down at the text screen.

Niko: *?*

Me: *I'm okay. Watching a movie with Chalice. I'll see you tomorrow.*

He sends me the thumbs up emoji.

"Are you mad about something?" I ask her.

She pauses the TV and turns to me. "Is this hot guy the reason you broke up with Thomas? Because if so, I have to ask why. You have been in love with him forever and he has been there for you since you came back. I really want you to think about what you're doing, what you're giving up." She stares at me.

Everyone on this island is fooled by Thomas' good guy behavior. But I won't lie for him to her, not anymore. "The answer to your question is no. I did not break up with Thomas for Niko. But I think he did make it easier for me to walk away from Thomas."

She shakes her head in confusion. "That's where I'm confused, why would you want to do that? What could he have done that is so bad?"

I go into the story about the night of our proposal and what Thomas asked of me.

"That fucking, con artist, flea bag, no good, bastard." Her islander inflection heavy in her anger. She picks up her phone.

"Wait, what are you doing?"

"I'm getting ready to cuss him out. Then, I'm going to call my brother to kick his smug face in. Then I'm calling the police on his illegal wanna be pimp ass."

I grab her hand to stop her. "Please, for me, don't. I haven't decided how to tell my parents. Besides, Niko. You're the only one who knows."

She presses her lips together and rolls her eyes at me. "Your dad is going to fuck him up too."

I sigh. Happy though, that she isn't looking at me with pity, but instead, revenge scenarios. I can definitely wrap my head around that. "Well, right now my parents already look at me in a way I can barely stand. I'm not ready to add this shame to the pot."

"Got it, sweets. You don't have to go convincing me about anything with these islander parents. So damned over protective and well meaning. Your secret is safe with me. But I still want to kick his ass. But I'll settle for giving you the biggest hug I can manage."

She leans over and wraps me in her arms. Warmth envelopes me, along with her sweet lilac perfume. I let go in her arms. When Chalice pulls away her face is as wet as mine.

"Men." We both say and laugh.

She restarts the movie and we get lost in the silence. My body lightened by my admission. One less thing to hide from someone I love. I should have told her sooner.

"So what are you gonna do about the hottie?" she asks.

"Niko?" I sigh. "I mean, nothing. We're just friends."

She turns her attention to me. I face the television.

"But, you said he kissed you. Twice."

I regret mentioning the whole kiss thing to her. I dare a glance and find her staring at me with stars in her eyes, which makes me blush.

"Friends kiss," I say, but even I don't believe myself.

"Not with a man that looks like that, and your fine ass. Be honest, you like him. It's okay to like someone that treats you well. And is dependable. And strong. And sweet. And damned sexy."

I blush more and my stomach tingles thinking about him. "I mean, okay I like him. But I don't think it's the right time to start something new. I'm dealing with a lot of shit, you know?"

Chalice throws a pillow at me. "I call bullshit, sweets. Love doesn't have a perfect time."

"Whatever. I never said anything about being in love with Niko." I roll my eyes at her. But my insides clench at the thought. Could I be feeling those sort of feelings for him? Isn't it too soon?

"Who said you have to be in love now? Get to know the man, that's all I'm saying. Have fun. Live."

This makes me smile. She is so right, she usually is. "You know who I do love?"

"Me?"

"You," I say.

We continue watching the movie. My mind wanders to Niko. *What is he doing right now? Is he thinking about me too?* A new kind of feeling forms deep inside of me—hope.

23

"*H*ow much longer do I have to beat this bag?" I ask Niko. "My arms weigh a ton."

He laughs while he watches me suffer. He doesn't answer me, so I don't stop, he's the trainer. Instead, he keeps going through his own series of pushups and sit-ups on repeat.

"Okay, that's enough for today," he says, and I don't hesitate. My arms drop to my side but feel like they may fall off.

"Thank goodness, Niko, you are so mean." I reach up to push him and immediately regret it. I wince in pain.

"It'll get easier, I promise. You think you can bring a fork to your mouth? I want to feed you."

I try to raise my arms and have to maneuver my body from side to side to make it work. "You might have to feed me." I laugh at how ridiculous I feel *and* look, but even laughing strains my limp arms. "Oh my goodness, and I'm meeting your cousin."

Niko puts his arm around me in a supportive manner, and we start towards the locker rooms. "Just wait till tomorrow, slugger; that's when the pain is gonna hit and you really won't be able to move. Double up on your water and if you think you can handle it, I can roll you out again."

The roller was the most painful thing I have ever experienced, each roll made me want to jump out of my skin. "Absolutely not. I will hydrate and start with a hot shower."

He walks me to the edge of the women's locker room and watches me until I disappear inside. It saddens me the way he treats me. Not because I don't like it, I do, I really do. It makes me sad because Thomas should be the one caring for me, helping me get stronger so that I can face the monsters that walk this earth.

My shower takes longer than expected with my noodle arms, and I have the hardest time reaching my head to secure my hair into a messy bun. If I had known of Niko's plan to turn my arms into wet spaghetti I would have chosen a simple dress instead of these skinny jeans that I can barely pull up and worse the lavender button up blouse with far too many buttons. He was definitely going to have to feed me.

When I walk out, he is waiting for me, looking too attractive. It is a challenge to keep the lines straight between us. We've already blurred them with kisses that fill my dreams. I don't want to be that girl though. You know, the one who jumps from one relationship to another. Then, I go back and forth about denying myself what my heart wants. Maybe Chalice is right, love isn't based on timelines.

Niko's smile grows when I cross into his vision, making me blush a million shades and causing a cheek-aching smile to take over my face. The butterflies in my stomach should be exhausted because they race around and crash into each other at the sight of him—who am I kidding, at the very thought of him. His hair is wet and tousled, his skin moist from a hard workout and hot shower. His fitted shirt reveals muscles I have an urgent desire to run my hands across.

I shake the thought from my head.

Niko pushes away from the wall and takes me by the hand. An act that is so simple, but for us is layered with meaning. For him he is showing me that he wants to be with me but cares enough for me to take it slow. Soft kisses, gentle hand holding. By accepting his hand I am showing him that I trust him enough to give him small pieces of me—that I'm trying to move forward.

My stomach knots when we round the corner on our way to the exit. Thomas is heading down the hall toward us. My first reaction is to release Niko's hand, but he holds onto mine instead of freeing it. I get it, why should I show Thomas any reaction at all; he deserves nothing from me—not even my acknowledgment. At least that is how I appear on the outside. On the inside, my heart is hammering against my chest. My eyes cloud. I can feel myself panic. Niko squeezes my hand and I stand taller. This is all Thomas' doing. He is responsible for the state of his life. Had he chosen to treat me like a human being, and someone that he loved, my hand would be laced in his right now.

His eyes fall onto our intertwined hands and when his eyes find mine they are heated with anger. He doesn't speak, he chooses to ignore us. My body tightens as he passes, unsure of what he might do once our backs are to him.

Niko and I continue forward.

I want to turn to see if he was behind us, if he was watching us, but I resist.

"That was awkward," I say.

THE RESTAURANT that Niko picks is a simple seaside bistro on the touristy part of the island. Niko and I make our way to the table, and he holds my hand the entire way. I'm happy with his choice of restaurant. I'd be lying if I said I wasn't thinking about the fact that locals rarely hang out in this area, unless it's for work. I'd like to spend a night with Niko that doesn't get back to my parents for a change. Not that it's their business, but the less I have to hear from them about my recent choices the better.

A beautiful woman with shoulder-length blonde hair stands up when we approach a table. She has to be Niko's cousin because the smile that crosses her face is megawatt. She comes from the booth and hugs Niko, then me. She is beautiful—fair skin, clear complexion, with a sprinkle of freckles, and a taller than average fit body.

We take a seat in the booth after an exchange of pleasantries—Niko and I on one side, and his cousin on the other.

"Oh my goodness, Whitney, you are gorgeous. Niko can't stop talking about you," she says, and Niko blushes.

"I'm not *that* bad," Niko says.

"Keep telling yourself that, cousin," she says and turns her attention to me. "Okay, so here's what I know. You're some type of child prodigy. You're an islander and very girly; not that that's an insult. It's just I'm such a tomboy. You're beautiful inside and out, strict parents, and deciding whether or not to move to London," she prattles off.

I exhale. Niko filled her in for sure. "Niko certainly chatted up my finer qualities, kept it to the good stuff." I have to wonder if he kept the other stuff from her for my sake or his. "Enough about me. What about you. How do you like the island?"

The server comes before she can answer and takes our order.

"I love it here. I mean, besides the sun, it's a lot of sun. I know I'm from California, but this is much brighter. The people are super nice, and I am enjoying spending some time with my cuzzo. I couldn't wait to meet his girlfriend." Her smile is hopeful, like she is seeing white gowns and bridesmaids flashing before her eyes.

I choke on my water. My eyes tear up. But I don't correct her. Sure, her words surprise me, but what's the harm in me secretly wishing it were true? Niko doesn't correct her either.

Sam is so easy to talk to that we all but leave Niko out of the conversation. Save the occasional comment, he is silent.

Dinner is over too soon. I really like his cousin. We promise to see each other again before she leaves.

Niko takes my hand, but this time he pulls me closer to him, so we're not just holding hands, but our arms are touching too. The feeling generated by such a simple act is everything.

Once we are both settled in the truck Niko turns to me instead of starting the car.

"I didn't tell her everything because I wasn't sure that was something you want everyone to know, not because of any other reason. Some stories are our own to tell. I'm proud of you, Whitney."

My eyes mist. He is always right there plucking the thoughts out of my head. "I don't understand."

"It was brief, your reaction, but I saw it. In the furrow of your brow, the breath you held," he says, reaching for my hands.

"Thank you...for explaining, I mean." I cross my heavy arms across my body. The cabin of the truck suddenly feels cramped. "I hate that I'm so quick to think the worst about myself. I was never like that before. In my session yesterday, Dr. Wesley—"

"—when did you start back?" Niko asks, he looks into my eyes; he is alight with happiness.

I shrug. "Recent development. You were right, though, I never should have stopped going."

"Go on."

"Well, my therapist, she is trying to make me see how much I've changed. But not just recognize the changes, embrace some of them, while releasing others."

"How do you mean?"

"I mean. For one, she said there is no way I can survive the I faced without being stronger. At first I didn't believe her, but I do see that I am stronger. If I was really a weak person, there'd be no way I would have made it out of there."

He runs his hand down my arm. "I'm happy you are able to see that in yourself. I know I do."

His comment makes me smile. "Thank you. We've also been talking a lot about fear and how it isn't all bad. Sometimes fear is actually my body telling me to be cautious. Did you know that in our brains there is a region called the Amygdala. I've been reading a lot about it and it's fascinating."

"You are fascinating."

I blush.

"So, this area of the brain, along with the prefrontal cortex and the hippocampus, can help your brain differentiate if something is a real danger or if something is as simple as a friend jumping out to scare you. What I'm learning is that after a traumatic event our brains can actually undergo a change. Can you believe that? I mean I'm still learning about all of this, and I'm giving you the dumbed down version. But, understanding this process is helping me process."

He gasps. "Did you just call me dumb?" his smile says he's joking.

"Of course not. But the neurology of the brain is not the most exciting conversation topic."

Niko leans forward and brushes my lips with the softest kiss I have ever felt, causing my body to tingle just about everywhere. "I am so happy to see you taking control over your life like this. I knew you were brave the second I met you. Whitney, you never cease to amaze me."

"Brave is not the right word for where I am right now, but I believe I'm getting there."

"I think you are further along than you think you are."

Where did you come from, Niko Andres?

24

NIKO

"You love her," Sam says when I let myself into her hotel room.

I shake my head at her. "I'm pretty sure that is a very strong word for how I feel for Whitney. Not sure it's love." I toss my keys on the counter, grab a beer out of the mini fridge, and fall onto the couch.

Sam sits down next to me. "Well, you may not love her, but you certainly like her—a lot."

My partner is someone I never lie to. It's a pact we have with each other—no lies, no secrets. "Whitney is phenomenal. She's smart and beautiful, and stronger than she knows. She has been through a fucking lot. So, I can't rush her."

"But you do love her?" she asks, walking to the fridge as well.

I take a long gulp of my beer and think about her question. When I see Whitney, I get anxious and nervous. When we're apart, I can't wait to see her again. I love any chance I get to touch her. And, my protective instincts awoke the moment I met her. "Don't know, never been in love."

Sam hands me another beer. "Until now," she teases.

"Stop. She and I are getting to know each other."

She laughs from deep within her belly. "You did not see the way you were looking at her at the restaurant," she sings the last word. "You hung on her every word."

Was I that bad? "Just forget about it. The second she finds out I'm not a personal trainer and I'm a cop, she's never gonna forgive me," I say as I suck down the second beer and let out a loud burp. *She's never going to forgive me.* "She trusts me. When she finds out I lied. Voop—" I sail my arm through the air.

Sam turns on the television. "You haven't given her a chance."

"Update me on Thomas," I say to get her to change the subject.

She turns to me, her face alight with energy and enthusiasm. She loves to work a case. "He is the biggest piece of shit."

"I know this already. The case?"

"He has been prying into my life. Most of his questions focus around my morality. He got handsy a few times, and I averted his attention easily enough. He hasn't come out and asked me to work for him, but the last time I talked to him, he said he had something big to discuss with me."

All I can do is shake my head. "He is desperate. You've been here a minute, and he's already propositioning you." Sam, I'm not worried about; she can handle herself. But Thomas' desperation makes me worried for Whitney. Desperate men are unpredictable.

"Has he talked about Whitney?"

"Not too much, but I'll feel him out. If I make him think I can do the work he wanted her for, maybe he'll forget about her."

I take another swig of my beer, stare at the tube, and mutter, "I hope so."

25

*T*here is so much I want to tell Dr. Wesley. I want to tell her about my growing feelings for Niko and how I think about possibilities with him, that I feel safe with him and how the growing feelings scare me. I want to tell her how much I am enjoying making plans for my future again. University College emailed me and I'm enrolled in classes for the Fall. She might think I'm on something, but I feel happiness coursing through my veins.

When I'm driving up toward the office building, I see a familiar form coming out of the door—Thomas. It's a medical office, so he may be seeing another doctor, but it's weird that he'd be here. I pull into a spot and wait for him to get into his car and drive off. His gait is cocky and overly confident as usual. I don't care if I'm late to my appointment; I can't risk him seeing me.

How long will my heart race at the sight of him? How long will fear course through my body? He has the power because I give it to him. Even if I resisted him, I know he is stronger than me and would just take it away.

I don't just wait until he's in his car and driving away. I wait until I can't see him at all—anywhere. Once he is out of sight I rush into the building and into her office.

I exchange pleasantries with Lucy, and wait. The ten minutes that go by allow me time to calm myself down after my near run in with Thomas.

"Good afternoon, Dr. Wesley. How are you?" I say when I walk through her office door.

"Doing just fine. And yourself?"

"Feeling better every day." I take my usual seat.

She smiles at me, but it's tense instead of her usual emotionless smile.

"How is the meditation going?"

"Better every day."

"Are you able to get through the entire session?"

I nod. "I am if I do it outside, not as easy if I'm inside."

She writes that down. "Why do you think that is?"

I shrug. I think it's because when I'm outside, when I close my eyes the sunlight filters through, I feel the heat on my skin and it lets me know I'm okay. But when I try at home it's too dark when I close my eyes, and I get freaked out."

She continues to jot what I'm saying down.

"Have you tried to turn on the light?"

I nod. "Doesn't help."

"I want you to keep trying at home. It's good that you have found a safe place to perform your meditation, but it is important that you feel safe enough to do it anywhere. Just in case you are in a situation where you can't get outside."

The thought alone makes me anxious. "True."

"Nightmares?"

"None this week. The sleeping pills are helping. I don't even have to take them every night."

"Good."

"Actually, I'm feeling a whole lot better. I'm starting to feel like my life is starting to fall back into place. I'm learning self-defense and it is empowering. I don't feel as afraid all the time."

She scribbles onto her pad, but remains silent.

"I was reaccepted at University College in London. I also met someone." I throw that in the middle, hoping it gets absorbed by everything else. "I guess, I'm starting to feel alive, doc. For the first time in over a year, I feel some of the old me working her way back."

Dr. Wesley doesn't speak. She only stares at me, her eyes assessing me.

"Say something," I urge.

She peers over her glasses at me. "You certainly appear happy," she says but doesn't smile.

"Is there something wrong with that? With me being happy? Because I thought that was the goal here."

Dr. Wesley removes her glasses. "My fear for you is that you glossed over some major steps in your healing process. You've avoided dealing with your issues, and you think running off to London will solve everything."

"What? I mean, I was always meant to go to school there. I look at it as me being back on track, or at least near the track. I can find another therapist in London. I don't plan on stopping."

She doesn't respond, instead she clears her throat and writes more.

"What steps am I missing?"

She flips the pages of the notebook and stops. "For starters, your fiancé."

I cross my arms over my chest. "I don't have a fiancé."

"Thomas," she says and slides her glasses back up to her face.

"What about him? He's a monster, and we aren't together anymore." I keep my voice even and flat.

Dr. Wesley closes and sets the tablet down on the side table. She stares at me before speaking. "I don't think things are as over for you two as you believe. He loves you, Whitney. And, you, you didn't give him a chance to adjust to what you went through."

I am out of my seat. "Are you kidding me? He wants time to adjust? What about my time? He didn't experience anything heinous, I did." *Is she for real?* "Wait. You're my doctor, why are you cheering for Thomas? I saw him before my appointment. Did he pay you to say these things?"

Dr. Wesley gestures for me to sit. I don't want to, but I need answers.

"He is struggling with not being with you. He misses you. He is sorry for how he's treated you. It's just that every time he sees you, he thinks of the horrible things that happened to you."

My jaw hits the floor. "Are you kidding me right now? *Thomas is sad and misses me? He can't stand what happened to me?*" My voice is loud and sharp. "That's what you're peddling here?"

She nods and purses her lips.

"I guess he omitted the fact that he wants to prostitute me out to make back the money he lost while I was gone." I jab my finger in her direction. How dare he hijack my therapist. How dare she be an unethical bitch when I trusted her. I knew I shouldn't have trusted a therapist that grew up with me on this fucking tiny-ass island. My first instinct was to find someone off island, a real professional that doesn't already know my life story.

Dr. Wesley waves my accusation away. "Preposterous. The Ackerly's are an upstanding family. There is no way their son would do something so unspeakable."

"Well he fooled you, too. Everybody on this stupid island thinks he's the golden boy. Maybe he was once upon a time, but I'm here to tell you the prince has fallen. He is a monster in the making."

She stares and waits for me to continue. "Whitney, please sit."

"I can't. This is so fucked up. I trusted you. *You* are a doctor. There are laws being broken here. You have an oath to do no harm. I would definitely call this harm. I knew this would be a conflict for you, knowing us both so well." I do aggressive air quotes. "But I thought you could be professional. Heard of a little thing called HIPPA? I'm pretty sure I could have your license for this."

"Please calm down, Whitney." She is out of her seat.

I stare daggers at her. "Calm down? Fuck you, Biance." She is no longer worthy of the title doctor. "Before I walk out of this office and never return, know this, you should consider a change of profession because you fucking suck at this one." I storm out with immediate plans of reporting her to the licensing board.

Damn Thomas. His desire to infect every facet of my life is exhausting. I need to beef up my training because I might have to kick his ass.

26

*T*oday is my first day back at my parent's house. I need to pack my room for my move to London. My therapy session was days ago. I sent a very long letter to the medical board about Dr. Wesley because there is no way she should be in practice.

I'm still upset with my therapist and Thomas, but my date with Niko overshadows all of the negativity in my life.

When I walk into the living room, Niko stands. He is stunning in his suit. My mind goes back to the first and only time I've seen him in a suit—the hotel suite. I shake the thought, even though I know we need to talk about his being in that room and what he was prepared to do had I not been the woman who walked through the door.

I cross the room and wrap my arms around him, and he plants a sweet kiss on my cheek, very close to my lips. I'm not hiding what we are becoming from anyone anymore.

My parents aren't warm, but they are polite to Niko.

"You look amazing, Whitney."

I blush at the compliment. "This old thing," I say. The dress is fitted, above the knee and midnight blue.

I say goodbye to my parents and leave with Niko.

Niko takes me to a romantic dinner club with live music. We sit close to one another and share a plate of appetizers. We hold hands, and Niko wraps his arms around me as we listen to the band's soothing sounds.

When we finish dinner, we walk to the beach. The moon hangs low and casts a glow on the water. I take off my heels, and we lace our fingers together, getting lost in the sounds of the waves.

I lean my head on his arm; I'm not tall enough to reach his shoulder. "Where did you come from?"

"You ask that a lot."

I stop walking and turn to him. "It's just my world was about to fall apart for the second time, and there you were. Here you are."

"I could say the same for you."

"Really?"

Niko lets go of my hand, gently cups my cheeks and neck with his long fingers and stares into my eyes. Only by the light from the restaurant patio am I able to see his face. "You kind of came out of nowhere, too. This terrified, gorgeous woman, begging for help. I fell for you in that instant."

He brings his face to mine and I dizzy when our lips touch. His tongue tastes my lips, requesting entrance and I don't hesitate to grant it. My body heats in secret places, and I long for more of this, more of him. When he breaks the kiss, I greedily pull him back for more. Moans escape me. Niko's hands caress my body, and I arch my back in response. He tells me what he wants with his mouth, with his hands, his panting breaths, and his growing erection. This moment could change everything for us.

We separate sooner than I want to, and we continue our walk on the beach. My heart beat slows, incrementally, calming itself from a very sensual display.

"So, if I tell you something, will you promise not to get mad?" I ask.

"No conversation that starts with that question is ever easy to promise."

"I know, but I don't want to keep anything from you, and I'm pretty sure you're gonna want to know this."

"How bout, I promise to try."

"Fair enough," I hesitate. "I saw Thomas the other day. He didn't see me, but I saw him."

"Okay."

"He was coming out of my therapist's building, and I hid in my car once I spotted him. He started seeing the same therapist as me. Long story, but I fired her."

Niko stops walking. "This has got to end. He can't keep meddling in your life. Over means over."

"I agree, but...I mean, I'll be in London in only a month. He'll never leave this island."

"Let's go." Niko says, grabbing my hand and leading me off the beach.

"I wouldn't have told you if it meant ending our date. You said you wouldn't get mad."

He looks back at me. "I said I would try and I'm not mad. I'm furious. He can't keep doing this to you. I won't let him."

Niko helps me into the truck. I'm suddenly exhausted. He climbs in the driver's side. He is bristling with anger.

"I had a lovely time tonight, Niko. Thank you." My face bears the sadness I am feeling. He is wound into my mess. My stress is his stress. I hate this.

He calms noticeably from my words. "I'm sorry. I have to keep you safe."

"I know."

Niko walks me to the front door. "I'm sorry I cut our evening short. It was one of the best nights ever. Every minute I spend with you feels that way. But this has to stop, Whitney. He can't keep harassing you and getting away with it."

I sit into one hip and pout. Here goes Thomas interfering with my life again. Over and over.

Niko brushes my lips with his thumb and kisses me on the lips. "Until next time, lovely lady." He kisses me, soft, slow. No tongue, just wet lips.

We say goodbye and I walk into the house. My heart sinks a little.

I hope he doesn't get into a fight with Thomas or worse.

Instead of suffering the worry of what he might or might not do to Thomas, I go back to packing up my room. I'm sure Chalice and Amaris are going to want to hang out with me tonight, since Amaris is leaving in a few days. That's another part of my life that I have recently enjoyed. Living with Chalice allows me to really enjoy my gals, like old times.

The house is quiet. Date night for mom and dad. I'll be long gone before they get back home.

27

NIKO

"Okay, this shit ends now. I need you to make your move with Thomas, now. I need him to back off of Whitney. He is a persistent fuck," I tell Sam when I stalk into her room.

She stares at me like I've gone mad. "And how do you expect me to do that. It's not like he's gonna just ask me to work for him; he doesn't know if he can trust me yet. And you went and pissed him off."

"That may be it. If he thinks he's gonna get back at me for stealing Whitney from him, he'll jump at the chance."

"Okay, I see where you're going with this. He is cocky and douchey enough to think with his ego," Sam says.

"Fuck it, I'm just gonna go beat the shit out of him. If he's in the hospital he can't fuck with her." I make my way toward the door.

"Niko, wait."

"What?" I don't turn toward her.

"That solves dick. If you beat him, you're off the fucking case. This is why you don't make things personal. You know better than this. If you beat him, that may save Whitney, but you know he will start this shit back up again once he heals. What about the other women?"

"Argh!" I shout. I pace back and forth, thinking. Another idea pops into my head. "Money problems. Confide in him that you are having money problems and came here hoping that I would bail you out, but you don't know how to ask me."

She rises from the bed. "I like it. I could say something about him being your good friend and maybe he could help me figure out what to say to you."

"Yes, and make sure you use the words desperate. He'll jump on that shit."

Sam goes to the fridge and grabs a couple of beers. She tosses me one. "You're pretty worried about her."

I sit on the edge of the sofa and nod. I take a draw of my beer and stare at the floor. "He is obsessed with her. She broke up with him and he has seen us together, but he is such a narcissist that he won't accept that she is no longer his. That makes me nervous. We gotta get him behind bars as soon as possible."

"Agreed. I'll call him right now."

I sit back and watch my partner go to work, using her sweetest voice as a lure.

"Got him," she says when she ends the call.

28

"Good Lord, sweets, I'm starving," Chalice says.

We take a seat at the food court. Our usual spot. I'm not superstitious. The likelihood of me being taken twice is as likely as me winning the lottery.

Chalice pouts. "I miss Amaris already, and now you're gonna be in London. You guys are leaving me and I'm never gonna see you."

I lean back in my seat. Then a thought comes to my mind. "Actually, that's not true. We've just increased your free lodging all over the world," I say trying to provide consolation.

"Hell's yes. I never thought of that. I'm gonna be booking tickets left and right."

I smile at my best friend. "I hope so."

She and I chit and chat about everything. She asks me about Niko and I gush. She tells me that she is cooling toward her most recent fellow, which I could have predicted. My friend needs way more attention than a long distance relationship can provide.

"Shut the front door," Chalice exhales. I look up to see she is staring at something behind me and has dropped her fork. I turn to follow the direction of her eyes and see what has her so shook. It's Thomas, and Sam. They are arm in arm, walking toward us.

"If he comes over here I am going to beat the holy hell out of him, Whit. I promise. Dumb ass wanna-be-fly-boy-bitch-ass-pimp." She is fuming.

I lean forward in my seat. "Just drop it, pretend I didn't tell you shit. He is nuts and I need to see what his angle is. With him, he always up to something."

"I don't know if I can, sweets." She pinches the bridge of her nose and I know she is on the verge of snatching her earrings out of her ears— full brawler mode. Tiny, but fierce.

"Play nice. That's what you have to do with fly-boy-bitch-ass-pimps." Her fly boy expression makes me smile. It's funny, yet right on the nose.

She isn't wrong though, I'd love to pick up a chair and smash him in the head with it. But I won't play my hand just yet.

"You forgot dumb-ass-wanna-be." She smiles, then mouths, "we can take him."

"I know." I mouth back and meet her smile. Inside I am not so cool. My heart ticks up in pace.

"Whitney, I thought that was you. I told Thomas here that I recognized you. Thomas, you remember Whitney," Sam beams her introduction.

"Yes, we've met," I say. "Small island and all. This is my friend Chalice. This is Sam." I almost say Niko's cousin, but hold my tongue because I have no idea what Thomas is up to.

"Do you mind if we join you?" Sam says as she sits. Thomas is eating this up with a stupid grin on his face.

Chalice, Sam and I chat while Thomas watches us. Watches me.

"You want something to drink or eat, babe?" Thomas says to Sam, but stares at me.

Babe?

Sam smiles, twinkly starry-eyed stares. "Sure, babe a blueberry smoothie."

They are in a relationship? She obviously hasn't mentioned this to Niko.

The second Thomas leaves I have to ask. "You and Thomas are a couple? You've only been in town a hot minute. Does Niko know?"

Her face is blushing pink. "Isn't he handsome. He is so ambitious and smart. He's starting a new business and he asked me to team up with him, so I may be staying around for a while." She nudges me in delight.

This can't be happening. Thomas can't have me, so he manipulates Sam, someone who is not even from this country? I have to tell Niko about this immediately. But first I have to warn Sam.

"Sam, did Thomas tell you he and I were involved?"

She turns her attention to me and then stares off after Thomas. "He may have mentioned you guys dated, nothing serious," she says.

Chalice pounces before I can. "Nothing serious? Thomas is a lying goat. They were engaged, and *he* is a monster."

Sam's eyebrows raise in confusion. I lean forward to whisper, but not before I double check that Thomas isn't coming back. "Get out while you can. Thomas is not what he seems. Chalice is telling the truth; he and I were engaged. It's also true he is sick. Your cousin had to help me get away from him, and his business will land you in a prison for prostitution. Run far and fast now."

Sam shakes her head. "I can handle myself. I'm sure it's not as bad as you say," she says just as Thomas returns handing her a smoothie.

"What's not as bad?" he asks.

"The food," I lie.

"We've got to be going, right Chalice?" I say moving my head in an exaggerated motion.

"Yes." She snaps to attention. "Before I open up a can of whoop ass," she says under her breath.

"Stay. Please. I was about to share with Sam, the role you'll be playing in the new business," Thomas says. The sneer on his face drips with hate.

He laces his fingers with Sam's, his dark brown, hers fair, but bronzed by her time under the island sun. I hate to leave her with him, but I have to believe this show is mostly for me.

"No thanks," I say, and Chalice gestures to her throat like a knife going across it, sneering at Thomas. I have to pull her along.

"Get away from him, he's a monster. You hear me? A monster!" Chalice calls out to Sam.

The second we are out of sight, I text Niko.

Me: *Were you aware that your cousin is with Thomas? Like holding hands and stuff?*

I don't have to wait for a response.

Niko: *No. I was not, but she won't be for long. Are you okay?*

Me: *Fine. Rattled, but fine.*

Niko: *Wanna get together later?*

Me: *I'd love to, but I promised I would spend the day with Chalice. I'll see you tomorrow at the gym.*

Niko: *Until tomorrow, then.*

I missed spending time with Niko. He crossed my mind throughout the evening. But I get to see him today. If I had my choice it wouldn't be for a workout. I want to get a different type of exercise. Then again, knowing Thomas has no plans of quitting, I better get tough and soon.

I hop out of the car at Milo's. I'm running late and Niko is probably already inside. I reach into my car, over my driver's seat and grab my phone and wrist wallet. When I back out of my door, I feel numbing pain in my head and all goes dark.

WHEN I AWAKEN, I don't open my eyes. Like before, I listen. I am patient as I attempt to heighten my awareness for any sounds that may give me a clue. The only sound I hear is my pounding heart echoing through my ears—lub, dub, lub, dub—set on repeat. I check my other senses. I don't think I'm outside. I feel air on my skin, but from an air conditioner, not the outdoors. The odor wafting through is familiar to me. I can't place it, but faint spice is the best way to describe it.

My arms are tied behind my back. I wiggle them to see how much room I have. Not much. My shoulders ache and my bindings bite at my wrist. What if Mason took me again? He promised retribution if we broke our promise of silence. But that can't be, I've been so focused on my own personal monster, I haven't had time to think about him much—save a nightmare or during my meditation.

There's no other option, I open my eyes. I survey what I know. With my hands tied behind my back, my ankles tied down, and a gag in my mouth, I may as well face my capture sooner rather than later. They have the power not me. My head is pounding with pain. The face I see when I open my eyes—Thomas.

"Look who finally decided to wake up. Bet you have a headache, eh? That's what happens to little teases like you." He walks around me, circling me like I'm prey.

"For a woman with your kind of smarts, I'm surprised you thought this was over. You thought you weren't going to be mine?" He laughs at the absurdity.

Deviant minds are the most mysterious minds on the planet. He has somehow twisted things around in his, and *I'm the bad guy*.

"Since you and that asshat, Niko, like story time so much, it's my turn to share a tale. Let me tell you a story about a stupid little stuck up, smart bitch."

He plops down on the sofa.

We are in his apartment. I look down for the first time and I am barely dressed, matching black bra and panties, barefoot. I close my eyes. There is no point in listening to his stupid story. He aims to kill me. It's the only way he gets what he wants. He'll probably dump my body and lead the fucking search.

Searing pain grips my cheek and spreads like wildfire up my face and down it at the same time. White light flashes and I push my eyes open. My blood curdling scream leaches through the gag. I am anger, I am desperation, I am sadness. The gun he struck me with in his hand. He wants to do worse, I can see it in his eyes. He hates me. He believes I ruined his life. My hot tears mixed with my blood leak down my face and drip onto my bare legs.

"I'm so sorry, baby, did I hurt you?" He snickers. "Eyes open and on me, I'm talking."

He sets the gun down and wraps his arms around me. "We still have time to fix this, Whit. You know what you have to do."

He pulls the gag from my mouth. "Scream again and I shoot you, understand?"

I nod my head.

"Can we start over?" he asks me.

I don't respond. Thomas gets close to my face and presses his lips to mine. The kiss is rough and unloving. My body shivers and my chest is aching from my heart beating so hard for so long.

This is it? After The Chamber, I thought, foolishly that I wouldn't have to suffer at the hand of another again, I mean not this way. The Chamber should have been worth a lifetime of pain. My story can't end here, with Thomas shooting me in the head. I can't help but wonder what my life would have been had I ran away with Connell.

I sob while Thomas sits back and watches.

"Whelp, I promised you a story," he announces.

I raise my head to look up at him. He is sitting in a chair right in front of me now. "Go to hell, Thomas," I say in a low voice.

Thomas doesn't react verbally. He picks up a hunting knife instead. "This beauty was a gift from dear old dad." He moves it around menacingly. "Story time, eh?"

Does he want me to answer him?

"I said eh?"

He picks up the gun and mashes it against the side of my head. Causing me to squeeze my eyes shut. I open them when his previous threat pushes into my mind. A whimper that I can't hold escapes me and I nod. Once.

"So, over a year ago I get a call from my girlfriend's father saying she's missing. I should have known something was wrong because the Alexander brood wasn't at the spring island party of the year. The engagement ring that sat in my pocket burned there. I was so lost in that moment."

He leans back in his chair giving me a chance to feel the pain he felt. I don't, my head and face are throbbing; I can barely focus of his words.

"The father and I pull our finances together to hire investigators to find her. I made risky business deals to get more money to find her. I lost everything searching for her. Then one day, like a miracle she's home. I didn't ask for much, just help getting back what she cost me.

I should have known she wouldn't go for it. She never loved me as much as I loved her. With talk of London she planned to leave, knowing this island runs through my veins. But the more time I gave her, the more I watched as she moved on without so much as a care about my well-being." He scoffs and lets out a laugh. "Your silly dates with the white boy, therapy appointments, meditation on the beach. I watched it all. I nearly shot you and Niko that night on the beach. You and your hand-holding, but you deserve a longer, more punishing death.

"I'll take him out first. Yeah, he won't be suspecting it. I still have access to him through his cousin. I'm heading to see him now. I asked her to have him meet us at Milo's. You know, so I can fake an apology for my behavior and ask his blessing to date her, like it's 19 fucking 29. Then boom! I'm going blow his fucking brains out." He shakes his head and laughs.

Suddenly, Thomas pops up so fast that I startle and fear causes my body to shake uncontrollably. He walks around the back of the chair and tilts it back and starts dragging me across the room. The chair leg gets caught on something and he loses his grip causing the chair to fall. I stifle a scream as my bound arms and hands meet the floor with force. He picks the chair and me up and drags me again into his bedroom.

"I can't look at you right now. If I shoot you before I kill your boyfriend it'll ruin the plan." He pushes the gag back into my mouth. "And don't think you can beg me to take you back once he's dead. I don't want you anymore. Besides, Sam will be a much better fuck than you. My business will soar with her, and she is down."

He rushes toward me, this time with his knife in hand. He pushes it into my throat. The sharp edge bites into my skin. I hold my breath, fearing that breathing will push the blade into my skin. The pain alerts me to my impending death. "I should slit your fucking throat right now. Let you bleed out all over my floor."

He releases the pressure, walks away abruptly and turns in the door way.

This man that I thought I knew so well is a monster in the truest form. There is no way that money changed him. This was inside of him all along. He stares at me, pure hate and loathing in his eyes.

Barely dressed. Bloody. Sobbing and shaking.

"Beautiful." He scratches his head and continues to stare at me. His eyes more crazy than sane. "Well, I better go, I have a blue-eyed devil to kill. You won't miss your boyfriend will you? Oh wait..." He rushes to my side. "Last part of the story." His voice is low and menacing. "You and me both know if he hadn't come in and saved the day, you'd be on your back right now fucking for me. You went upstairs, Whitney. Think about that during the little life you have left."

I buck against the ropes and growl. I hate him and there isn't anything I can do but wait here until he decides when it's my time to go.

Tears blind my vision, but I watch his wavy image get further away, and then the door slams. A million things race through my mind. Niko and I had a gym appointment; surely he will be worried enough to look for me.

There's no way he'd agree to meet Thomas for Sam; he hates Thomas. Unless it's to tell him to back off; that is something he would do. Why would Sam agree to be his whore?

I have got to get out of here. I try my ropes again. To my surprise, the wood makes a cracking, whining sound. *When I fell?* It strained the wood, there is so much more give. I go to work on the ropes.

30

NIKO

I hope Whitney isn't too put out by my running late. She didn't answer my text when I messaged her. Sam and I meeting about Thomas ran long. That fucker really thinks Sam is gonna start seeing clients for him. She is scheduled to meet with her first client next weekend. Personally, sooner would be better. Thomas presents a danger to my girl and needs to be off the streets immediately.

"Hey, Milo."

"Niko." Milo smiles and me.

"Whitney already back there?" I ask.

He shakes his head. "Nope. You beat her this time. It's pretty empty back there."

Strange. I'm like thirty minutes late. I jog to the back of the gym, and when I don't see her, I check the women's locker room. I'm sure it's nothing, but panic runs through me. I run past Milo shouting, "If you see her call me!"

"Will do," he calls after me. "Everything okay?"

I don't answer. I keep calling her phone as I scan the parking lot for her car. I didn't see it when I first arrived, but I wasn't really looking for it because I assumed she was already inside. I pace the storefront. I call her number again and I hear a ringing sound close by. I hang up and dial her number again. I follow the ringing to the source. Her smashed phone is sitting behind a parking bump.

Fuck me.

I dial two numbers—Sam and the local police. Time to blow my cover and find my girl. Something is wrong.

Sam and the police arrive within minutes.

I give them the info I have. Sam and I share our true credentials with the police. It's the only way. I need help finding her. There could be another explanation for her phone, maybe she lost it—but Thomas' face is all I see.

"Milo, I think something happened to Whitney. Can I review your cameras?"

He eyes the law enforcement credentials now hanging from my neck. Hurt flashes across his face but he recovers quickly. He nods and I follow.

"I instruct the young wide-eyed officer with the deep brown skin and his partner. "Get a hold of her parents and have them come down here now. Also, we need to track her car."

The young cop speaks. "She isn't missing yet. She could have lost her phone."

I walk up to him and get close. "She has a stalker. Something is wrong. I feel it in my bones."

Everyone moves. Sam and I follow Milo to the room with the camera.

We look through the tapes and all gasp at the same time. Thomas took her. He knocked her out, threw her into the back seat of her own car. We watch him look down and pick up her belongings, except her phone, he kicks it—in broad daylight.

My heart is pounding. I am scared to death.

Sam puts her hand on my shoulder. "We're gonna find her, Niko. This is what we do."

But she knows time is ticking away quickly.

Whitney's parents walk into the room, confusion and worry mark their faces. Whitney shares so many similarities to her mother, which makes a sob catch in my throat.

"Mr. and Mrs. Alexander. There isn't much time." I show them the video recording.

Whitney's mother falls into her husband arms in hysterics. Another emotion takes over her father—rage. "We trusted him with our daughter."

I send Sam to find out the location updates of the car. Even I know I can't just run around the island like a crazy man. We need solid clues.

"I came to Barbados as a part of an international task force when Thomas showed up on our radar. He was opening up a prostitution ring and he was trying to convince Whitney to work for him," I inform the Alexanders.

Whitney's mother breaks away from her husband and runs, her grief too much to contain. These poor people have only had their daughter back a few months.

"I'll kill him," her father says and looks me dead in the eyes. He means it.

"We'll get her back. I love your daughter. I'll die saving her if I have to."

Mr. Alexander nods his understanding.

I take off after Sam and he goes after his wife.

Minutes feel like hours before we get the report of her car.

"Niko, the car has been traced to Thomas' apartment." The look on Sam's face bares my feelings. His house is personal. He means to kill her. Sam and I head to the apartment, along with every available cop in the area. Whitney's parents hitch a ride in an accompanying squad car.

31

WHITNEY

I use all of my might to stress the splintered wood of the chair, each sound of fracture is a gleam of hope. *Whitney you can't die here. Your story can't end here.* With each tiny cracking sound the ropes feel looser. I stop in my tracks when the bedroom door flies open. Thomas drags me into the living room.

"Change of plans. Your boyfriend and the cops found you," he says and walks in haste to the window. "Ha. The whole police department is here. Don't they know you're not worth all this fuss?" He stares at me, venom pouring from his eyes, spooking my soul. If I survive this I will have new nightmares. Thomas will now be the star.

"This whole circus because you betrayed me. Cause you couldn't fuck for money, when you fucked for free for a year."

I squeeze my eyes tight in an attempt drown out his voice. I have one mission, get free. Thomas' phone rings and we both jump.

"This is Thomas Ackerly, how the fuck may I help you?"

He is silent while he listens.

"Oh, no, she's alive...for now. I have no demands. I made them months ago, and no one listened. So, when you hear the first shot, that's me putting a bullet in her head, and the second shot is the bullet I put in mine. I'm about to murder suicide this. Sounds poet as a motherfucker, don't it?" He hangs up.

The ropes give. My hands are free, but I don't move. Thomas and I are locked in a tense stare. He puts his attention to the window. The knife is close to me. I could reach for it, if I can get my legs free. Thomas starts talking and peering at the window. I go to work on the restraints on my legs, which aren't tied tight at all.

There is no time to waste. For a brief second I remember the gun in his hand and have no doubt that he wouldn't hesitate to put a bullet in my head. This is my only chance.

I reach for the knife, it's heavy.

He is talking out loud to Niko, monologuing through the window about how he is going to kill me, so cocky he doesn't hear me or feel me coming. He is enjoying the show.

"Hey, Whitney. He turns to me and I shove the knife into his stomach. The gun discharges before it falls to the floor. The sound is deafening, my ears ring and I have to resist the urge to cover them.

Shock and pain mar Thomas' face, once handsome and loving, now the face of the devil. I cry and shake but push forward and reach for the gun. I've never held a gun before or stabbed someone. I can't be a victim anymore. Thomas staggers forward, holding the handle of the knife with one hand and reaching for me with the other.

Not taking my eyes off of him, I back up.

My hands shake. My body quivers. Still, my eyes never leave his.

Vomit crawls up my throat. The gun burns my hands. I toss it down the hallway and step back, until my back slams against the front door. Our eyes are locked.

Thomas is deciding, me or the gun. He starts to pull the knife out and while he is focused on that task, I throw the door open and run. Thomas is on the sixth floor. I push for the elevator, praying for it to open. I turn to the sound of Thomas stumbling out of his door. He spills into the hallway, ignoring his pain, fueled by hate. I make it through the stairway door as the second gunshot rings through the air—it's aim, my head.

I am blinded by my tears as I steadily run down, down, down. So many stairs.

The door above me slams against the wall; he's inside the stairwell with me. My heart leaps into my throat. In my panic I trip and fall down an unknown amount of steps. Thomas leans over the side. He is only a couple floors above me. "You stupid bitch!"

I roll out of view as Thomas fires more shots. My broken body doesn't want to work, but I can hear his heavy breathing. I will myself to get up. He is hurt, but he is coming. I hit the first step of another flight, on and on I run, nearly falling so many times, but I can't die here. I can't die by his hand.

Sunlight. It breaks through the window of the first floor. I know Niko is out there. I know the police are out there. I break through the door and run as fast and hard as I can. Ignoring my pain, ignoring my fear, ignoring every sensation.

Strong hands grab me. I scream and I fight, I hit, I kick, I scream as loud as I can so Niko can hear me, so he can find me.

"Whitney, it's me. I'm here, you're safe."

I open my eyes and I am in Niko's arms. "He's coming!" I scream over and over.

Niko squeezes me in his arms and someone brings a blanket and covers my body. He takes me away from the scene.

The door to the building crashes opens and I turn to find Thomas winded but pushing forward like a robotic assassin.

"Freeze!" the police yell.

He doesn't see but they are coming out of the building behind him; they are on the side of the building. He is out of options.

"Whitney, if I can't have you. No one can!"

He raises the gun in shaky hands and gun shots ring out. Thomas collapses to the ground.

The next moments are a blur of ambulances, my family, Chalice, Niko.

Everything goes dark.

32

*M*y body screaming in pain tells me I'm alive. I open my eyes and see my parents on one side of my bed, and Niko, Sam, Chalice, and Amaris on the other. Ironic, this is probably what they expected the first time I was taken by a stranger, for me to be found but in bad shape.

"Baby. You're awake," my dad's voice rings through the silence. My dad never cries but when I look into his eyes they flood with tears.

"What happened?" Daddy asks.

Using the controls to raise the bed slightly, I wince where my body aches. At least four bodies lurch forward to assist me.

"Niko and I had a workout appointment at Milo's Gym. I was rushing, not paying attention to my surroundings. Pain and then darkness. When I woke up, I was bound and gagged. He was planning to kill Niko, then come back to finish me off."

My family reacts in a series of gasps and cries.

I continue. "My opportunity came when he dragged the chair I was tied to across the room. He dropped me and the chair broke. That's how I managed to free myself. I stabbed him with his with his own knife and ran as fast as I could, dodging bullets." Tears rush down my cheeks from recalling my brush with death.

"Thomas was a sick man. He had everyone fooled," Daddy says.

"Thank God you're okay. I don't know what I would have done if we lost you," Mom cries.

She kisses my cheek.

"I'm okay, Mom."

I glance around at my family while I wipe the newly forming tears. "Guys, can I talk to Niko alone, please?"

All eyes turn to Niko. I can see hesitation on my dad's face. But he gets up first, and everyone follows. One by one they file out of my hospital room, but they touch or kiss me on the way out.

Niko moves to the seat closest to me. I can see in his face that he knows what's coming—what I'm going to say to him.

"So, you're a cop?"

He looks down.

My heart breaks a little with the admission of his lie. This whole time.

"Is Thomas dead?"

Niko looks up and stares into my eyes. "This should have never happened to you. I should have protected you. I should have been there. I'm so sorry."

He feels guilty for not protecting me. But he shouldn't, protecting me isn't his responsibility. After my brush with death, It's mine. I know that now.

"Funny, before a few minutes ago, before I told you guys what happened, I thought I was a victim. I laid in this bed feeling sorry for all the things that I've been through. But I realized something."

"What's that?" Niko asks.

"I saved myself. I was my own hero."

We sit in silence, then he smiles. "You did."

"Is Thomas alive?"

Niko takes a couple of deep breaths. "Yes, unfortunately for mankind, he is. Recovering from your stab wound and gunshot wounds."

"Here?"

He nods his head. "Two floors up. Surrounded by guards."

Two floors is all that separates me from the man that tried to kill me. If I hadn't broken free, I'd be dead right now. I saw the look in his eyes, raw hate. He wanted me. How long will he be put away? Is he going to come after me again?

"Do you hate me?" Niko asks, breaking through my thoughts.

"No. I could never hate you. Just disappointed that you never told me." I look away from him. It's true. Other than the lie, he has been good to me. "You were going to arrest me when we first met."

He sighs. "Part of the job. My cover can't be revealed to anyone, unless something like this happens and the job requires it."

"Is Sam really your cousin?" I know the answer as the question tumbles out of my mouth.

He shakes his head. "No, she's my partner. I called her to help because I was becoming distracted and I couldn't allow the case to be compromised." He presses his lips into a hard line. I'm not used to seeing worry like this on Niko's face. He usually wears a smile that lights up the room.

"With what?"

"Falling in love."

Oh my goodness. Did Niko just say he is falling in love with me? What am I supposed to say to that? How am I supposed to feel after knowing that he lied to me?

"You love me?"

"Very much."

"Why do you think you love me? Thomas said he loved me too and look how that turned out."

Niko moves onto the edge of my bed. He is cautious when he sits. "I don't think, I know. I've loved you from the moment you crossed the threshold into my hotel suite. Scared and trusting. Beautiful and brave. In the midst of everything you were facing, everything you had faced, you were hopeful. I thank God every day that it was me in that room with you. Your heart is strong and beautiful."

I gaze into his eyes and think about all of the things he just said to me. If only I saw myself the way he sees me.

"So, was everything you told me about yourself a lie? A back story for your job?"

Niko leans closer to me, taking my hands in his. "All true. I have citizenship in all the places I mentioned. I currently live in England and so does my family. The only thing I didn't tell you was that my folk's divorced when I was younger. Mom remarried and my step-dad is amazing, and I have a brother and sister. My dog's name is Dreamer. I love the beach and coffee. You know me, Whitney. My job is different but that's all."

"That's a lot of missing information."

"Not really. I promise I planned to tell you."

I turn my head away from him. "It's not the same, Niko. You were the only person who knew me. When I walked into that hotel room, I gave you something of myself that no one else had—my truth. The dark truth of what Thomas wanted from me. Somehow you managed to earn my trust under circumstances when I should never trust anyone again. I let you in and felt things for you I've never felt for anyone else. I thought I loved Thomas, until I fell in love with you." I pause at my own realization. "I loved you. I was starting to carve a space in my future for you."

Niko smiles when the word love pours out of my mouth, but his expression changes as I put my feelings in past tense. *How can I trust this man again? How can I see a future with someone I don't entirely know?* He lied.

"You know what keeps going through my mind?" I ask.

He shakes his head.

I smirk. I can't believe what I am about to admit. Again, Niko is the only one I'd ever admit this to. "It's actually something Thomas said to me when I was gagged and bound."

Niko's face bares the pain he feels hearing those words. "I will never forgive myself for not being there to keep you safe."

I give him a weak smile and squeeze his hand.

"What he said settled into my bones and I don't know if I will ever be able to remove those chilling words from my mind, partly because I have asked myself the same question repeatedly."

I pause before I continue, sharing this will break me down into the tiniest pieces of nothing. Tears start to fall and a sob escapes me. Niko has me in his arms, consoling me. I let him.

When I get control of my emotions I push myself from his chest and he lets me go. Worry marring his beautiful eyes, now a stormy blue.

"What he said was that I went into the room. I went up to the sixth floor of the hotel and that the only reason I'm not on my back right now is because you were there." I break down again.

"I don't believe that, Whitney. You shouldn't believe that about yourself. You shouldn't worry about that either. We'll never know because it didn't happen. Neither you, me, or that monster will ever know."

All I can do is wipe tears from my face and listen. Maybe he's right, but Thomas' words dug deep into my soul and pulled out what I think I've always been thinking, feeling. Sure, I'd whack the errant thought away, but it would always revisit me.

I look into his eyes. "It's the reason we can't be together, Niko. I have to be on my own right now. It's time for me to learn that I don't need my parents, my friends, or a man to survive. I have to know in my core that I can save myself, every time. If I don't, his words will haunt me."

Niko looks down at his hands, and he doesn't say anything. I wait for him. When he finally looks up at me, the sadness in his eyes nearly breaks my heart. I don't want to hurt him. I don't want to lose him, but I can't lose myself.

He forms a small smile. "You're sure about this?"

I nod. My heart is pounding in my chest and my stomach hurts. This might be the biggest mistake in my entire life.

"What kind of man would I be if I fought you on something so important to you? I only want what's best for you." He leans forward and the single best and worst thing happens. His lips graze mine. He pulls his face back and gazes into my eyes and I give him permission to kiss me again. Tender gentle lips meet mine and I match his desire for our last kiss to be memorable. His tongue dances with mine and tears stream down my cheeks.

"I love you, Whitney." He brushes his fingers across my eyes, wiping my tears and caressing my cheek. I close my eyes and savor the contact, suddenly feeling aged by my life.

Niko walks toward the door and turns toward me before he leaves. "You take care of yourself," he says and walks out of my life.

33

*A*fter three days in the hospital I finally get to go home. When I come out of the ensuite bathroom, Sam is sitting on a chair. A small plant in her hand.

"Hi," she says.

"Hey."

I continue packing up my things. My parents are due to arrive in the next hour or so. I told them not to rush because these things can take time.

"How are you feeling? You look good, love," she says in her British accent.

I smile at her compliment. She seems uncomfortable in my presence. Is it because she lied too? A lie coming from her doesn't touch me in the same places. "Thanks."

She stands and shifts her weight from foot to foot. I stop what I'm doing because she obviously has something to tell me.

"Look. I know how it feels when someone you care about lies to you. But in our line of work, it is par for the course."

I take a seat on the edge of my bed. My body still aches in places. I shrug at her comment.

"You think Niko planned to fall in love with you? I don't think he has ever been in love with anyone."

I sigh. "I care about him too. Probably too much. But I need time to work on myself."

"I can understand that. You deserve as much time as you need." She looks down at her feet before continuing. "Look, he doesn't know I'm here. I mean, I don't care if you tell him I stopped by. He's taking it hard, losing you. I just want you to know that he is an amazing guy and he's worth the risk, Whitney. If you love him, I mean really love him, don't let him slip away."

If she only knew how many times I've wanted to pick up the phone and call him. Text him. Tell him that I made a horrible mistake. I miss him so much. Not just as someone I was becoming romantically involved with—I miss my friend.

"Yeah, I know. Niko will probably be my greatest regret." I sigh.

"Don't be a stranger when you get to London. Maybe we could meet for drinks. I could show you around," she says.

"That sounds nice." It would be nice to know someone out there, but I know I won't be strong enough to look her up, knowing how easy it would be to see Niko again. Amaris offered to move with me, but I declined. Having her there would be another crutch for me to lean on, and I need to learn how to depend on my own legs to hold me up. A thought pops into my head.

"Can you do me a favor?"

"Anything," she says.

TWENTY MINUTES LATER, I'm standing at the foot of Thomas' bed. Sam kept telling me on repeat that Niko was not going to like this, but I can't leave this country, or this hospital, without facing Thomas. He is big part of this journey. There are two officers at his door, and one inside. Thomas looks small handcuffed to the bed. He is broken, bruised, and bandaged. Shot and stabbed—but like the cockroach he is, he's still alive.

"Hi, Thomas," I say.

He only stares at me. Sam backs up and positions herself by the door. I pull up the empty chair near his bed and sit down. The room is thrumming with tension. "I'm getting discharged today, but I couldn't leave without saying goodbye."

Still, he doesn't speak. He stares at me and blinks.

"I wanted to share a story with you. I know how much you like them. It's about a little genius girl who was snatched from her precious island. From everyone she knows and everything that she loves. While she was gone, she was forced to have sex with strange rich and powerful men. Guilt and fear wrecked her body and mind every moment. The worse part of all was at the end of the year, the strangers weren't so foreign to her—she was beaten up by the guilt of her body and mind's adaptation to her new life. She hated herself for not hating it." I start laughing at the absurdity of this story. Thomas' eyes grow with worry. *I can be crazy, too.* "The thoughts that saved her were knowing that she had a loving family, her beloved island, friends, and a man that loved her."

Thomas looks away.

I get closer to him. "Oh, no you don't Mr. Ackerly, eyes this fucking way. The story is about to get good."

He turns back and looks at me.

"Imagine her dismay when her boyfriend finds out his love is back from hell, and instead of loving her and keeping her safe he thinks it's a fancy idea to treat her like a whore and offer her up for fast cash to get himself back on top. Can you imagine that?"

I glance over at Sam.

"Thankfully, her love was a dumbass and his first client was a cop," I say and belly laugh this time. "Imagine that. The poor genius girl thought she was saved. But things for her get so much worse. The man she thought she loved wasn't just the worst prince charming ever, turns out he was actually the devil himself. He repeatedly harassed her, got inside of her therapist's head, and then kidnapped her. Boy, was he surprised when she stabbed him with his own knife." I stand up, my story is almost over.

"Like I said, I know how much you like stories. This one is coming to an end—but it's full of twists and turns. Karma is a bitch because if the guy would have been a good person, a loving human being, you know, the poor little genius girl would have gotten around to telling him about the four million dollars she was paid by her captor. That kind of money would have fixed all of his problems. I'll let that sink in." I say and wait. His face contorts and his brows furrow. "Good, you understand what I'm getting at. Really good story, right?"

"Whitney—" he tries to say, but I cut him off, putting my hand up.

"So here it is. I'm moving to London for school. I'm telling you this, so if you ever get out of prison, you'll know my last known location. But just know that some of my fortune will go to training myself to be a lethal fucking bitch, so if assholes like you even look at me wrong—you'll regret the day you were born.

I start to walk away. "I hope you liked my story, and I hope you burn in hell with my blessing." I smile from ear to ear and walk out of his room. Of course I start crying, I'm not a complete cyborg, but damn it felt amazing to take a little of my power back. I can feel it in my posture, my shoulders pulled back a bit more, my head a little higher.

I hope to be as fierce as the woman in that room, and for the first time, I believe with time I will be.

By the time we get back to my room my tears are all dried up.

"Woman, I am in awe of you. I wish Niko could have seen you back there. You were amazing." Sam hugs me.

"Thanks. That felt pretty damn good. I think I will meet up with you for drinks after I get settled in. If I can do what I just did in there, who knows what else I can do."

"Perfect. I better get out of here. Hey if you're ever in the mood for some of London's finest brew, Unlax is tops. Niko introduced me to it; it's his favorite coffee house. There's only one, so it's easy to find."

We hug again and she's out the door. I know what she did there. I shake my head and smile.

34

LONDON, SIX MONTHS LATER

*T*he last three years of my life have come to this place. *London.*

I really hate thinking about the past and all the twists and turns I made in my life that I could have done differently. Not feeling guilty about the choices I can't change is a valuable lesson that I learned from my whack job therapist. *But,* I am human and I can't help but wonder if I wouldn't have taken the two-year break in the first place and come straight here, would any of this even happened to me?

When those thoughts come crashing into my head, I quickly push them out. I have to because the reality is: It happened to me, it all happened and unless someone comes up with a time capsule to go back and change the past, I can't.

Even if I could, I don't know if I would. Because after everything that I went through, I'm different. I'm changed, but surprisingly, the outcome isn't bad. The road to get here sucked in all ways possible, but I am a survivor and I wear it like a badge.

Before The Chamber I would have never taken combat classes, and now I can't get enough of them—jujitsu, Krav Maga, weapons handling, you name it. I am inhaling the knowledge. My body has lost the baby softness and that has been replaced with early signs of sleek warrior. I found a therapist and she is amazing. My sessions with her are helping me work through the grief and guilt of my too recent past.

I changed my doctorate degree to Security and Criminal Science. A choice, born from my experiences, I want to help others. If I can get a Thomas off the streets, or even better, a Mason, using my genius brains and education then I have to; it's my purpose. Of course my parents' imaginations' got the best of them and they envisioned me with a gun and cuffs out running down bad guys. I relieved their worried minds when I informed them that I will be tracking them from the comfort of a computer screen—at least that's the plan. The best news is that it'll take me less than two years to complete.

I miss my family and the island. But I don't miss the sun as much as I thought I would. London's fog calms me in a way I hadn't expected.

When I'm still and quiet, I can't help but think of Niko. Is he here? Or is he on another assignment? I miss him. I forgave him back in the hospital for the lies. I will be forever thankful for his friendship. In more ways than I care to admit, he saved me. Time and time again. In big ways and small.

I know I did the right thing by letting him go, he deserved so much better than what I could give him back then. I was broken *and* beaten, both physically and emotionally.

It's still hard to believe that it's been six months since I left home—it feels like a life time—circa London, is what I like to call that time in my life. That me wasn't ready for him or any man. It wasn't fair for me to start a relationship with him when I didn't even know who I was anymore.

These days, I'm feeling more myself than I have in a long time. But, I don't feel like my old self, I feel like my new self. A stronger more confident me, aged by circumstances and experience. I love how I feel in my bones. Being kidnapped two times was two times too many. The woman that I've become will make it nearly impossible to play the victim to the whims of a man ever again.

Next week I start an exciting internship in the school crimes division, with school shootings growing rampant, it is too important. My dissertation is what actually landed me the internship, a solution for school crimes may be implemented one day. The focus of my dissertation is decreasing bullying, identifying children that are isolated, and at risk in order to decrease school violence.

I can't think of a better place to start than with kids. It's so strange that I'm only going to be twenty-two, barely older than a lot of high schoolers—yet I feel twenty years older than them.

This meeting with the company I'm interning with is a big deal, so I decide to dress the part—a simple white blouse, gray dress pants, and gray heels. My hair is knotted into a messy low bun with tendrils framing my face. I'm wearing nude make-up, except for a soft pink lip gloss. I throw on my gray winter coat, purple scarf and matching gloves and head out the door.

There are eleven people that I count situated at a conference table, in cushy black office chairs, waiting for the speaker to show. I'm more nervous than I should be. Being a prodigy, I'm accustomed to being the youngest in the room by a decade or two. Small conversations are taking place around me, while I wonder what the hell is going on with my body.

When Niko walks into the room, I know it's because of him. He stops at the front of the table. His chocolate hair is brushed back, neat. His blue eyes find mine but they don't register as much surprise as my own. My smile threatens to split my face.

He begins his presentation.

A story of him being a kid that was small for his age, an easy target for bullies. He tells the story of how he turned his life around, by motivating the entire school—the same small fish concept he uses with adults, the tattoo he bears on his forearm. Save the small fish before they become sharks.

When the story is over the room erupts with applause, no one louder than me. I am so proud of Niko. I love him. I feel it through my soul. My body yearns for him. When his eyes find mine, I smile wider and brighter than anyone else.

I stand back and watch him at the end of the meeting as he shines, engaging in smaller conversations. This crusade of his is just what the world needs right now.

When the people begin dispersing, they take the air with them. We are alone.

Neither of us speaks for several moments.

Niko is first. "So, what did you think?"

My cheeks hurt so much from smiling. "So amazing, Niko. More than I could have expected for my first internship. I'm all in." The fact that we get to work together is another bonus.

"Really?" he asks, unsure of himself in a way I've never seen.

"Yes," I nearly squeal.

"I need coffee. You?"

I don't hesitate. "Absolutely."

Niko extends his hand and I take it, like second nature or a second skin. Butterflies pepper my stomach in a way that only happens when I am in his presence.

UNLAX, is a quaint coffee shop with heavy, dark furniture. We sit on the same side of the table.

Like a couple of dorks we stare at each other and blush, a lot.

"So, how do you like it here?"

"I love it here. I never thought I'd be okay without my sun, but this is so much better. I can open my eyes all the way without sunglasses. I'll appreciate my sun more when I go home."

When the waitress comes to our table she addresses me first, "For you, madam?"

Niko perks up. "May I?" he asks me, and I nod his permission.

"The lady would like a coffee, with enough cream to make it caramel in color, and two sugars."

I can't help but smile.

"And the gentlemen?"

I chime in before he can answer. "He'll take his black." I turn to him. "You still take it that way?" I ask.

Niko reaches out and puts both hands on either side of my face. His lips take me hostage and hold me there. He licks and tastes me, sucking my lips, our tongues one. I look up at the waitress. "Cancel that order."

I pull Niko from the table and out of the coffee shop. I scan the street until I find what I'm looking for. He doesn't ask any questions; his smiling face is all I need to push me forward. I want this more than anything.

I pull us through the lobby of a small hotel that is beautiful and ancient. I take out my cards and rent a room for the next two days. I don't know what plans he has, but he'll have to cancel. I fumble with the key giddy with excitement. Out of all the things I've wanted in my life, nothing is more important than this moment.

Niko rescues me from the key and opens the door. I begin unbuttoning my shirt before he can get the door closed. Not caring, I pull and rip the remaining buttons. He stands and looks at me with awe, shock, and concern. My chest rising and falling. My skin heated.

"Niko, why are you dressed?" I pant.

"Why aren't you? What are you doing?" he asks.

My face falls. *Shit, did I misread things?*

"Niko, I'm sorry about what happened back in Barbados. I wasn't the right girl for you then. But I am now. I don't hate myself for the past. I don't blame myself anymore. I've been training in combat and weapons. I live all by myself, and I'm not afraid of anything but not being with you. I miss you. I love you so much that it hurts." I start to panic because he hasn't moved. I pull my blouse up over my shoulders and stare into his eyes, pleading for him to want me. The thought never crossed my mind that he might not. How badly did I hurt him? Did he meet someone else?

"Niko. Please tell me I'm not too late." It is nearly a whisper.

His expression changes and he stalks toward me. He doesn't touch me, but he's close enough to. "You don't know how long I've waited to hear those words come out of your mouth. am going to make love to you right now and when I'm done, I will never leave your side again. I love you so much, Whitney Alexander."

My heart floods with happiness, and I nod greedily for him to take me. Niko peels his clothes from his body, and then removes mine. "My God you're exquisite. Everything I imagined and more." His eyes cover my flesh. I do the same. His manhood is impressive and ready. His skin stretches over the dips and grooves of his muscles. My heart is racing, and my breathing is out of control. I work out all the time, but this is carnal and hormonal.

Niko lifts me into the air and I wrap my legs around him. I devour his face with my lips, I pant with lust and hunger. He pulls the blanket off the bed and lays me down.

"I don't have anything with me. I mean, I don't carry protection in my wallet." His laugh is mixed with embarrassment and amusement.

"You mean you're not sixteen?" I laugh. "I'm on protection, a shot I get every three months. We're covered." I hate that my mind drifts back to the reason I began that stupid shot, Mason. Will he ever not be a thought in the back of my mind?

Niko's expression changes. It's time to get what my body has been craving.

"I love you, Whitney," he says and studies my body, making me crazy inside. When he finally sinks inside of me, I nearly scream from the feeling, the fullness.

His tongue dances with mine and we find a rhythm.

"You feel so good," Niko says into my mouth.

All I can manage is a moan in return.

My body moves in ways foreign to me as he pushes deeper inside of me, rolling his hips and making my head swim. With a full hand of his ass, I pull him deeper still and nearly come apart.

"Woman, I never want to be anywhere but inside of you," he growls before he pulls out of me, leaving me cold with want. His eyes hold mine.

"Marry me, Whitney?" he asks and his eyes never leave mine.

My heart sinks into the depths within me. I want to ask if he just said what I think he did, but I know what I heard. My mind betrays me and goes back to my last proposal, and I have to shake my head to clear it. The love of my life is hovering over me, bearing everything, stepping out on a line and taking a chance on me.

I raise up and push him down onto his back and straddle him. Niko stares up at me with wonder in his eyes, waiting for my next move. He gasps with surprise when I sink down onto him, taking all of him. With eyes never leaving his, I roll my hips in slow circles.

"Niko Andres, can I have you like this anytime I want?" I ask and grind harder. His eyes open to the size of saucers.

"Yes," he says around a moan.

"Can I climb on top of you and do this?" I lift off and slam down, over and over, contracting my walls around him. I lick and bite my lips with satisfaction when he shatters inside of me. Taking all of him, I push until he is as deep inside of me as I can get him and my body comes apart, contracting around him like a vise.

"Yes!" I shout while my body joins him in our joined ecstasy. "I will marry you."

He pulls me into his arms, our moans and breaths are a love song. I see lights as we continue to explode into a crescendo of sounds. Fiery sensations run through me.

Thoroughly spent, I collapse onto his chest.

35

When I wake up, I am disoriented. I look around and realize that I wasn't dreaming. I have no idea the time. Based upon the look of the sky through the sheer curtain, it must be daytime. Niko is not next to me in the bed, but this is the hotel we checked into, so I didn't dream this. My naked body another indication that I'm not dreaming. But where is Niko?

The room door swings open before I can think too long about his whereabouts. My beautiful man walks through the door carrying a carafe of coffee and a bag of what I'm hoping is food, because I'm famished.

"You said yes."

"I did." I hop up from the bed and grab his undershirt from the floor. It is enormous on me and smells of him—clean, with a minty hint, mixed with Niko. I can't resist the urge to pull it into my hand and breathe in, not even bothering to hide the warm smile that covers my face. His scent is home to me.

When I look up, Niko is watching me. "I fucking love you too much. Do we have a tattered and worn robe to put you in? Because seeing you in my shirt is doing things to me."

I laugh at him, shaking my head as I go in search for my panties. My goal right now is singular, and it's to get my hands on whatever is in that brown bag, and if it isn't food, I might kill my fiancé. The word dances though my mind.

He reaches into the bag and pulls out two bagels, cream cheese, and danishes, placing them on plates on the table.

Niko pulls out my seat for me. "So, what have you been up to in London?"

This makes laugh. I grab my coffee and take a sip as I sit back and watch him. He is mine. My chest vibrates and hums with excitement.

"What did I say?" he asks, smiling.

"It's just funny that we're engaged and you are asking me that."

His face falls. "Don't even let your mind go there. You already said yes."

"No one is changing their mind. I know I said yes, and I meant it. I love you and marrying you." I take a sip and moan. It really is divine. I sit back and study him before I answer his question. We do have a lot to discuss.

I sigh. "Did Sam tell you about the money? The four million dollars?" I ask. We may as well get that out of the way. She may have kept it a secret from him, hoping I'd tell him one day, but I highly doubt it.

He nods. "She did."

"And what do you think about the money. I mean me accepting the money?"

He shrugs. "I don't know what I think. Was there a way to return it?"

"I don't know. The money was just there. I never planned on touching it, until that night upstairs in the room when I met you, the night you planned to arrest me."

He sucks in air and lets it out.

"I was happy for the money that night because I was able to use it to save myself, or so I thought."

We sit in silence and stare at each other. He doesn't say he has a problem with the money, but he also doesn't tell me he thinks it's okay that I have it.

"Listen. I'm not going to give it back. I couldn't if I wanted to. At first, I thought it was dirty money, but not anymore. It's mine. I didn't ask for it. But I won't give it away either."

Niko smiles at me and raises his hands. "Not asking you to. I'm good with the money as long as you are. You shouldn't feel guilty or dirty about it."

I exhale and smile at him. Thankful that he wasn't judging me.

"Back to your question, I am renting a two-bedroom flat in Belize Park. I thought about buying something but at the time, that seemed too long term." I nibble on the pastry and sip my coffee before I continue.

"Apart from that, I've been going to school and taking a bunch of fighting and weapons classes. I bet I can take you."

He laughs. "You think so? We'll have to see about that."

We sit in silence and enjoy our breakfast.

"What have you been up to? You didn't seem as surprised to see me as I was to see you."

His eyebrow hitches up. "You caught that?"

"I'm much more observant these days. Being kidnapped twice has taught me a thing or two."

Niko's expression is wary when I say that. "I knew you were here the second you got off the plane."

"What? Are you serious?"

He nods. "And, don't get mad, but...I've also been by your flat, multiple times. And I've watched some of your training sessions. And, no, you can't take me, yet. But you are well on your way." He lets out a small laugh. "I wasn't surprised in the conference room because I was given a list of everyone that would be on the task force. Imagine my surprise when one of the interns turned out to be you."

"You've been spying on me?" I cross my arms across my chest. "Why?"

He puts his food down. "You've been kidnapped, not once, but twice. Two times, Whitney. I've never been in love before, and I didn't stop loving you just because you didn't want me. I watched you to make sure you were safe. New country and surroundings and all. But I was so proud of you. Watching you learn to kick ass. I spoke with your trainers and told them who you were to me. I know that you smile from ear to ear when you leave your therapy sessions."

"I can't believe it. I'm engaged to a full-fledged stalker," I say, but a smile tugs at the corner of my mouth. "Why didn't you reveal yourself to me back then?"

"You weren't ready for me then. Are you mad?"

I smile at him. "Are you kidding? My very own vigilante, superhero. Of course not." How can I be mad at him when he only wanted to keep me safe?

"Want to know the craziest part?"

I nod.

"Around two months ago, I got scared," he says.

"Of what?"

"You not needing me anymore. I could see you changing. You became more aware of your surroundings. I actually thought you saw me a couple of times. I could see your confidence in the way you walked and held yourself. I watched you become a badass. Your Krav Maga instructor told me you were one of his top students. He said whatever happened to you in the past fueled you. I started panicking. I begged Sam to arrange a meetup," he admits. "Of course, she refused. She said it had to happen organically. I was so mad at her."

"I'm listening."

"Nothing else. I told my mom and both my dads about you. They can't wait to meet you."

I stare at Niko. I'm wearing my new perma-smile. I deserve the happiness that is right in front of me. "When is that going to happen?"

"How soon can you get dressed?"

36

*T*hirty minutes later, Niko and I are standing in the middle of my flat. I walk over and open the window that overlooks my lush backyard.

"So what do you think? My lease isn't up for another six months. But there is definitely room for two." I walk towards him. "I mean, unless you want to live apart. Are you old fashioned?" I wrap my arms around him and tilt my face up, hopeful for a kiss.

His lips are warm and sweet. I moan into his mouth.

"I can have my things moved in by tomorrow."

"Really? I'll make room for you in the closet." My cheeks hurt from smiling.

"That's settled. Now go shower and get cleaned up before I have my way with you again. You have parents to meet." He turns me toward the bedroom and smacks my ass.

"So bossy," I say smiling all the way to my bedroom.

Twenty minutes later I step out of the room, wearing a pair of slim fit jeans, a deep gold sweater, and knee high flat boots. In the six months that I've been here, I haven't figured out my hair. The curls are less defined, with a frizz that has a mind of its own. Messy bun has become my signature look. "Am I parent ready?"

He reaches out his arms for me, and I cross the room eager to fill the space between them. We stand in the center of my living room holding one another.

"Are you really mine?" I ask, pulling myself as close to him as I can.

"All yours, forever." He kisses top of my head. "And you?"

"You had me at bad ass."

This causes him to laugh. A sound that has an invisible cord that travels to my heart.

"My badass."

"Okay then it is settled," I giggle. "I'm a badass, and I'm yours. You are mine. I love you more than coffee and life and now I get to meet your —" Niko drops to his knee and looks up at me, cutting me off before I can say family. "What are you doing?"

"I'm making this official. Whitney Marie Alexander, will you marry me?" Niko slides a ring box in front of me. Inside is a simple, yet elegant solitaire with two smaller clusters of diamonds on each side. I look from the ring to him and back to the ring.

"It's beautiful. When did you get this?" I ask. This is really happening. Excitement courses through my body and mind.

"Today, while you were snoring. There's a jewelry store right next to the coffee shop. Let's just say I don't waste any time."

"Yes, Niko, I will marry you."

I hold out my finger and he slides the ring on and sweeps me into his arms, flooding my face with kisses. "You don't know how happy you have made me."

When he sets me down, I push him playfully. "I don't snore."

"You do, and I can't wait to wake up to it every day for the rest of our lives."

"I hate you," I say through a smile.

Niko laughs and wraps an arm around me. "I know. Let's go meet my parents. They are going to love you."

We leave our flat arm in arm, with me swearing that I wasn't snoring and Niko promising to record me. One thing that he said keeps replaying in my ears the entire ride. He can't wait to wake up to my alleged snoring every day for the rest of our lives. Even though he obviously heard something else—the rest of my life with Niko Andres is something I will cherish and forever be grateful for.

WEEPING VIOLET EXCERPT

Chapter One

How can I be afraid and excited at the same time? On one hand, I'm free. Mason kept his promise and let us go. In style, too. I'm sure the private plane and escort to our front doors had more to do with him and his control than it does with concern for us. But here I am, rolling down the road in the back of a luxury sedan on the way to my house. I missed my mother so much while I was gone. I'm almost more afraid to see what my disappearance did to her. She already suffered the loss of my father, and now this. Maybe calling her first would be a better option?

I've been counting the minutes, hours, and days to my release, but I never thought about what it all means for me or for her. *Shit.* What about my best friends Tabitha and Taron...and Logan? What about him? Did he move on and find someone else? Could I blame him if he did? No, I can't. I've been gone a whole year.

The closer we get to my destination, dread and fear replace my excitement. I have to remember my new mantra. I open my journal that has been sitting on my lap this whole ride and I scrawl the ten words that have given me strength since I boarded the plane home. *I am safe. I am strong. I am a survivor.* I close my eyes and take deep breaths; we are close to home.

"Miss, we're here," the driver interrupts my attempts at calming myself down.

I glance up at him and offer a tight smile. My heart is racing and slamming against my chest.

I turn and look at my home. It's small and sweet, just like I remember it, with bright spring flowers and a neat, manicured lawn. I stare down at the words I have written in my journal—my salvation during the last year. I filled it with my fears, my secret wishes, and dreams, and my growing inner strength is revealed between the lines. *I can do this.*

This is it. I am going to hit the reset button. *Home.*

It's time to forever shed the label of Violet the sex slave...the Chambermaid...whatever I was during the last year, and become me again.

Once I ring that doorbell, I step back into my life as Brinley Avery Bishop—college student, daughter, and aspiring actress. *Girlfriend?* Maybe I should follow my agent's advice and dye my naturally blonde locks. I could do a vibrant red, or even a deep brown. The color doesn't matter. The point is, if I look less like *me*, I will feel less like *her.*

My legs are lead as I climb out of the car and make my way up the short path to the front door. With sweaty palms, I reach for the bell. My only thoughts are for the woman on the other side and what her reaction to my arrival is going to be. Mom must be out of her mind. I can't imagine what she suffered—waking up one day to learn that her only daughter is missing. I'm sure by now she believes I'm dead. How else could she mentally survive?

What am I going to say to her about my absence? What will be enough for her? What will be too much for Mason?

Too much time has passed.

Still, I have to do this. This is my home and we are the only family the other has. With shaky hands, I depress the bell and I wait.

It feels like forever.

My chest feels heavy and tight. My body is teeming with nervous energy, so much that my hands tremble. She'll have questions. How will I answer them? Mason was dead serious when he made his threat to us: "Breathe a word of your whereabouts, or what took place here, and you will see me again."

It's not like I even know where I was. He made sure to blindfold me during my arrival and my departure. Mason did his job well. No one used their real name in The Chamber, not even me. So what would I say? There is nothing that I could add that would help anyone locate the place.

What Mason doesn't know is that he has nothing to worry about. All I want to do is forget about my year of being passed around from stranger to stranger as they used my body for their own pleasure. I am the last person who would run around broadcasting what I went through. The sooner I can put it all behind me, the better—but, somehow, I know I will never forget.

When the door flies open my mother and I just stare into each other's green eyes. She looks older. Her eyes lack their usual brightness. Her blonde hair lacks its usual luster. I probably look *too* good. During the last year I was kept in impeccable shape and condition through regular spa treatments, my own personal groomer, and massages. That's another thing I'll have to explain to my mother. Of course, one would expect a kidnapping victim to look beaten or bruised, worse for the wear, not like she just stepped off a photo shoot.

"Brinley." The word is a whisper. She gazes at me like I'm a ghost from her past.

I grab my mother into my arms. She folds into them and we both sob in the doorway. I don't let my mother go for what feels like forever. I don't want to. She is home. Seeing her, holding her, is my only proof that I am home and free.

"Come on. Let's get you inside, honey."

My mother takes my hand and doesn't let it go. I follow her inside on unsteady legs and take a seat on the sofa because I lack the strength to stand at the moment. On my long plane ride home, I thought of all the things I would say to my mother. Somehow, all of those words have evaded me. I feel like a stranger, like a cloned version of myself. All of a sudden, I am a sci-fi experiment. I look like Brinley. I sound like her, too. I even have her memories. But something feels different, because I am not the same. I'm tarnished and forever changed because of The Chamber. How can anyone experience an entire year at the hands of a cunning and sadistic monster and not be ruined and broken? Even the strongest among the seven of us will struggle when she gets home.

I gaze around the house where I grew up, and it pretty much looks the same as it did a year ago. My mother has always preferred a minimalist approach to decor. There's a sofa, a television stand, a small flat-screen television, a bookshelf she made from recycled materials, and her abstract paintings adorn the walls. I remember when she first picked up painting. I teased her and said, "Just because you purchase a blank canvas and acrylic paints, it doesn't make you an artist." But looking around at them now, after a year of missing her and my home, I realize her paintings are masterpieces. They are to me because they're an integral part of our home.

My mom is a hippie who has always believed that a house is meant for eating and sleeping, and living takes place outdoors. Camping, hiking, biking, sightseeing, or gardening—any activity that gives us the opportunity to convene with nature—is what we should spend our valuable time doing.

She returns with a glass of water. I hadn't even noticed that she'd left the room. I take my time sipping my water and tasting it. I savor the simplicity of a drinking a glass of water in *my* home. I glance over at my mother and see that her face is wet with tears. Mine is, too. Suddenly, the water has to compete with the lump that has taken up residency in my throat.

"I can't believe you're here!" she blurts out before taking me into her arms again. There is no coffee table to set my glass on, so I hold onto it and her. We cry big, sorrowful, relief-filled tears onto each other's shoulders. "I am never letting you out of my sight again. Do you hear me?" She breaks our hold and begins checking me in earnest. "Where have you been? Are you okay? Are you hurt?"

"Define 'hurt,'" I say, wiping my eyes.

"Please tell me what happened, Brinley. Where were you?" She wipes her eyes.

I take a deep breath and begin to tell the last story I ever want to repeat. The worst part is that I know this won't be the last time I have to tell it. There will always be questions. The hardest part is figuring out the equal balance of what I can tell her without landing myself on Mason's hit list, while keeping in mind that she's a mother who has been without word from her child for a year.

"I decided to go for a morning run near school," I take a long draw of my water. "I know that I should have listened to Logan. He said it was not safe for me to be running alone, especially in Hollywood. But you know me. You always said 'Stubborn' was my middle name.... Mom, do you happen to have anything stronger than water?" *I need liquid courage before I can keep going.*

"Sure, baby." She pops up and quickly returns with a bottle of Pinot and two wine glasses.

I guess we both need something extra right now. I take my full wine glass and practically down it. It only takes a couple of minutes before the alcohol makes me less anxious.

"Like an idiot, I left my dorm and my friends, and I took off on a run toward the GPO by myself."

"The what?" Mom asks.

"Seriously, Mom? The Griffith Park Observatory. I didn't think anything of it, really. I mean, I always thought the freaks came out at night, you know? But that was the day I learned the freaks never sleep." I take another long draw of my wine and finish it. My mother refills my glass. I don't hesitate to take another sip. "I made it to the GPO in record time. I was feeling that high I get from running. Then I bent down to tie my shoe, and before I could get back to my feet again, I saw three men coming for me. I didn't even have a chance to run, scream, or fight. They were on me before I could process what was happening. They put a cloth to my face and that was it. Lights out for me."

My mother finishes her first glass and pours another. Tears are rolling freely down her cheeks. I can't visibly see her hands shaking, but I hear the bottle clank repeatedly against her wine glass.

I continue. "When I woke up, I was on an airplane."

"Where did they take you?" Her voice catches on a sob.

"I have no idea. I thought for sure I was headed to my death. I had no reason to believe otherwise. I mean, only psychos would kidnap perfect strangers. I just knew I was going to die and we'd never see each other again." I pause and draw in two deep breaths. This is the tricky part. What I say from here on could get me into a lot of trouble if I believe Mason's threat, and I do. "What I learned after I got off the plane ride was that death would have been the easy way out for me,

Mom. Death would have meant peace. But when I got off of that plane, I never thought I would know peace again."

My mother tries to stifle her heavy sobs as they rip through her, but I can tell she has never been more scared than this moment, hearing my words. My living nightmare.

"The place I was taken was a sex club for rich and powerful men. I was forced to work there, and...I'm sure you can figure out the rest."

"Oh my god! Oh my god!" My mother pulls me into her arms. Her cries are loud and frightened. "We have to call the police." She squeezes me.

"And tell them what?" I pull away from her so I can look her in the eyes. She needs to understand that calling or telling anyone is not an

option. Especially the police. "The man who took us warned us that if we said anything, he'll come after us. He said we wouldn't be safe anywhere on earth. He will make us suffer. He's a dangerous man. Trust me. The men who take part in his annual chambers will do anything to keep this covered up. Let it be over. Isn't it enough that I'm home?" I beg and plead with her.

My mother grabs my arms and shakes me a little. "You listen here. I don't give a rat's hairy ass about this monster. He took you, kept you for a year, and made you do unspeakable things. He has to pay. He has to be stopped." Her voice is sharper than I've ever heard it.

I jump up from the sofa. I have to get through to her. "This is a losing battle. You don't want this. What if he takes me again? Just drop it, Mom! When I first got there he showed us videos. He watched us for two years before he kidnapped me. He's probably watching me now. I have the money. I just want to forget." Tears are pouring down my cheeks.

I just want her to understand, I don't want to look over my shoulder. I want to live my own life, free of The Chamber. Free of The Monster. I need to work at living my new life. I hit the reset button and now I need to find my new normal.

"I just want to get past this, Mom." I am exhausted.

"What money, Brinley?" she asks.

"Four million dollars," I say. My voice is just above a whisper. I know she is going to freak out. I mean, if I was a mother and my daughter was telling me what I am telling her, I would freak out, too. "I know you have to call the police and tell them I'm home. I know they will want to talk to me and ask me questions. But I can only tell them the bare minimum." I continue to speak in a low, unsure voice. "This is the way it has to be, Mom. It's the only way I can be here with you."

"I can't believe what I'm hearing." My mother jumps up from the sofa and starts pacing. "I don't understand. Why would you have four million dollars?"

I flop back down on the sofa. I bring my knees up to my chest and bury my face into them. At this point, the only way I can speak to my mother is from this position. Discussing any aspect of my time in The Chamber is exactly what I wanted to avoid. It was the most humiliating and embarrassing year of my life. I know that showing up on my mother's doorstep, after being gone for a year with no word or communication, an explanation can't be avoided.

"I don't know, Mom. We *are* talking about a crazy person here. He kidnapped seven of us, made us have sex with a bunch of rich guys for a year, then paid us millions for it. Crazy is not meant to be understood. Crazy seems to have the power to do whatever it wants." I knew this would be difficult for her. How can I expect anyone to understand what I went through? I know—with the exception of the six other girls, my sisters—no one ever will. I'm not happy that I was paid, but I'm not going to give the money back. It won't change what happened to me, or to any of us. I left a sex chamber a millionaire.

The worst part of all of this is how confused I feel. When I first arrived at The Chamber I wanted to die—to curl myself into a tiny ball and fade away to nothing. But an experience like that changes you. The Chamber was nothing like I expected it to be. I wasn't chained to a wall. I wasn't kept in some dank, dark cell. I wasn't beaten or drugged.

It was quite the opposite. I made friends with the other girls. I had massages and manicures and movie nights. I had my own personal trainer and groomer. The only time I felt like I was in hell was when I had to perform sex acts with strangers who, by the end of the year, weren't even strangers to me anymore. All of this knowledge, coupled with the money, makes me even more confused, and makes my experience even harder to fathom. Anyone I tell the full details of my story to would think I'm crazy, too. The first question that will spring forth in their minds will be, "Why did you stay?" As if I had a choice.

Personally, I don't know why Mason is worried about us telling anyone. I never want anyone to really know what happened within those vast walls.

What would I say, anyway? *Well, Mom, I had sex with thirty-five different men. Thirty-seven if you include the times that Mason had his turn with me, or the times I fell asleep in my Chamber, and my personal guard, Gabe, came to visit me.* Why should I feel guilty about the money? I know it won't buy me my sanity, but that much money will help me start my new life—especially when I don't even know who I am anymore.

My mother watches me with concern in her green eyes. I hope she can see *me*. I'm the same little girl who loved acting and making up stories since I was in grade school. I'm the same girl who wanted to finish college and travel to New York with my boyfriend, Logan, and attend Juilliard. And even though I am not quite as hippie as she is, I hope she still recognizes the me who saw the beauty in the mountains, the trees, and the ocean. I am praying that as she gazes at me with confusion and concern, *I* still exist in her eyes, because I may need her help to find myself along the way.

When my mother scoots toward me on the sofa, I am surprised and relieved when she grabs me into the most loving and protective embrace I have ever felt. We both sob again in each other's arms. She may never understand what happened to me, but she loves me, regardless.

"We will get through this together, baby," she promises. I am so overcome, I can only nod. There are no words.

Mom calls the police and she agrees with me that I can tell them whatever I feel they need to know to keep us safe. I don't mention the money to them, fearing it will raise too many questions that I cannot answer.

I'm beyond exhausted; fortunately I manage to get by only sharing the bare minimum with the officers—the location from where I was snatched, the fact that everyone in the place I was kept used a fake name, that I only saw the outside for the first time today. I told them that I traveled a great distance by plane, but have no idea where I was being kept for the entire year. My mother sobbed quietly while I spoke to the officers, who could only tell me how lucky I am to be alive. I see a look on my mother's face that worries me. It's a combination of fear, pity, and sadness. She tries to mask it, but I catch a glimpse before she can turn away.

One of the officers gave us his card in case I remember more. If only they knew just how much I remember. They also gave my mother some information on places I can go if I need emotional help. And just like that, they were gone. I hope I don't receive any more visits from the police. I am willing to bury any memories of the last year. If I am lucky, my name and case will get filed away under unsolved crimes.

My room looks just like it did before I moved into the dorm two years ago. I feel like I'm back in my last year of high school. My walls are plastered with the heartthrobs of that time and my many photo collages from high school. I was really into pastels my senior year. My room looks like an Easter basket exploded all over the walls and floors.

All of my belongings from AMDA, the American Musical and Dramatic Academy, are back in place in my room. Damn, I had a sweet spot in the bungalows, too. I'll bet my friends and teachers all think I'm dead. Whatever. I'm too tired to think about my life. I hope my mom calls Logan for me, if he is even still in Los Angeles. It was bad enough just popping up on her doorstep after all this time. I can't do that to him. That thought frightens me. At least if she calls him first and gives him time to process the fact that I'm home, he won't have to stare at me like a ghost come back to life when he sees me. As much as I can't wait to see Logan, I fear the look in his eyes.

What if he has moved on? He could have a whole new life, complete with a girlfriend by now. *What if he has a girlfriend?* I can't be upset with him if he does. It's been a year. *Snap out of it, Brinley. If he moved on there is nothing you can do.*

Today I will sleep and recharge. Tomorrow...life.

When I stare down at my bed, my stomach becomes queasy. The light purple comforter thrusts me back to The Chamber and my life as Violet. I run into my bathroom and deposit what little I have in my stomach into the toilet. Closing the lid, I sit on top of it and run cool water into the sink. I don't fight the tears that stream down my face. I have grown accustomed to crying this past year. *You will be okay, Brinley. It is just a color. It doesn't define you. It never did. You are a survivor. You wouldn't be here if you weren't.* I grab a towel, dampen it, and wipe my face. I gather myself, walk back to my room, and remove the comforter. I drop it in a heap in the hall outside of my room and shut the door on any memory it might force me to recall of Violet.

I pull a quilt from my closet, wrap up in it, and lie on my bed. Right away, I feel the pull of sleep. My body is spent from a very emotional reunion. I am almost out when my mother knocks on the door.

"Honey. Sorry to disturb you, but I saved these for you. I knew you would come home to me."

I glance up and see that she has a stack of journals.

"I planned to give them to you for your birthday last year. I know how much it helped you to write in them when Dad died. I just thought maybe..."

I sit up in my bed and take the journals from her hands. She plants a kiss on my forehead. After everything, being home still doesn't feel real. I think I'm numb. I stack the journals on my bedside table. "Thanks, Mom. I think I can use them." She's right, and she knows me well. When my father died a year after he was stricken with cancer, my journals were the only thing that kept me sane. I let it all out on paper—the anger, the fear, the pain. I did the same in The Chamber.

"Would you rather talk to a professional?" she asks.

"How about I try these first, Mom?"

"Okay, baby. What do you want me to do with the comforter? Was it dirty?"

"Throw it away. I don't like purple anymore."

"Will do. Let me know if you need anything." She heads for my door. "I love you."

"Love you, too, Mom."

I think I'm asleep before she closes the door.

Chapter Two

One by one, we are named—branded like cattle. We're all given names of colors or objects that represent a color. Raven, Sunshine, Flame... The Monster has literally stripped us down to nothing, destroying our souls and essence.

My heart is beating in my throat as he makes his way down the line toward me. There is no escape. I can only stand here and suffer my fate. I watch in horror as five antique bookcases slide open along the circular wall, revealing hidden staircases. Five girls slip into the darkness and the bookcases close behind them.

Then there are two—me and the dark-haired girl standing to my right. I can feel her fear because I share it. Mason, The Monster, wants to have fun with us. He flashes us his serpent-sized erection, and I almost pass out. He calls us his "two virgins."

Mason named the other girl Flame. She and I are led to another area. With every step we take, I'm closer to having a full-blown panic attack. She must be just as scared. The only thing keeping me from collapsing is the picture of my mom that Mason showed me and what he told me would happen to her if I don't cooperate with him. He has me, and he knows it. I would never sacrifice my mother for a very slim chance to escape.

We follow a blonde named Ivory down a series of corridors and tunnels. Her white stilettos clack loudly against the stone floor. I look around at my surroundings and see that we are in a castle-like structure with high ceilings and stone walls and floors. With each echoing step, my head aches more and more. We turn the corner, and come to a door with a sign that says: DEFLOWERING CHAMBER.

Shit. Ivory ushers Flame and I through the door. There are naked guards on either side of the entrance. Their erections are at attention, for us, I assume. It doesn't seem like we will have a choice about what happens next. I want to die. I don't want to do this. I don't deserve what is about to happen. Neither of us do. Tears fall heavily down my face. I have never been a fighter.

The room is stark white. The only color accent comes from the blood-red and lavender pillowcases on top of two of the three beds.

Tyson and Gabe, two guards who have also flashed us their enormous erections, come into the room. Tyson leads Flame to one bed, and Gabe takes me. I don't fight or try to run. I should, but where would I go? I do as I am told. Before I have a chance to prepare, Gabe removes my clothes and lays me down on the bed with the lavender pillows. His tongue begins to sweep over my sex. He takes his hands and pushes my legs as far apart as they will go. I squeeze my eyes closed as tight as I can. If I hold my breath maybe I can make myself pass out, or better yet just stop breathing entirely. Relentlessly, he sucks and licks until I feel something come over me. Heat floods between my legs as his tongue pushes forcefully inside of me.

I lose my train of thought and focus only on the feeling down there. An unwelcome moan escapes my lips naturally. I am a woman with hormones, and with every lick and suck, my body betrays me. When his lips latch on to my clitoris, I come undone. The intensity of his relentless sucking is unnerving. I scream out and my body explodes with violent, uncontrollable shaking. Gabe doesn't stop. He is unyielding with his punishment. He drives his fingers inside of me. I try to scoot my body back away from him, but my efforts are pointless. I feel my innocence tear away from me as he continues to thrust his fingers inside me and devour me with his tongue until I come apart again.

He stops. "You are fucking amazing. I will take extra special care of you this year," he says before walking away.

"My, my, Violet. Your personal guard sure did warm you up for me." I open my eyes and see Mason, The Monster. His dark hair, nearly black eyes, and fair skin symbolize pure evil to me. He looks to be in his thirties, and for the briefest second, I wonder what makes a man decide to kidnap women and run a place like this. It doesn't matter what his motivation is. I hate everything about him. To me, he will always be a monster.

He is completely naked and I see that the large snake between his legs is prepared to strike. I dare a peek at the other bed and see that Flame is busy with her guard. Mason doesn't give me another second to react or prepare. He flips me over onto my stomach and pulls me up onto my knees, causing my back to arch with his exaggerated pull. My breath escapes me when he slams the entire length of his erection into me. He isn't patient, he isn't kind—he is a wild animal, a real monster. He pounds into me relentlessly—impaling and filling me inside over and over. I am distracted suddenly by the sound of screaming. It is loud and horrific. I seek out Flame, but she is not screaming. She looks like she's enjoying herself. *Where are the screams coming from?* Someone is utterly terrified for her life and needs help...

"Brinley. Brinley! Wake up." Someone calls me from a distance.

I feel arms around me. I thrash, trying to break free of the binding arms so I can help the screaming girl.

"Brinley, it's okay. You're home. You're safe."

I open my eyes to Logan, and realize the screams are mine. I've had my first nightmare.

"Oh my god, Logan!" I cry out and fold into his arms. I break down into heavy sobs. His hold is strong and protective. "I was back there all over again."

"You're safe, babe. I promise."

He rubs my back and it is immediately soothing. It's the first touch from a man I've welcomed in a year. I'm so relieved it was a nightmare and I'm waking up to Logan's strong embrace. It felt so real.

"When did you get here?" I ask.

"Your mom called me after you went to sleep. I couldn't wait for you to wake up, so I have been here for a few hours."

"Doing what?"

"Watching you sleep."

I gaze up at him and see that his blue eyes are red-rimmed.

"I thought I lost you forever. I died a little every day that you were gone." He squeezes me.

I hope he's right. I really hope that I am back. I don't know how much of me I left behind.

"Are you thirsty? I can get you water or juice," he offers.

I panic. "No. Don't leave me. Please." I feel the remnants from my dream tugging at me. My entire core is shaking.

"Never." He kisses the top of my head.

I fall onto my side and Logan follows suit, holding me. "Where's my mom?"

"She went to the store to get food for you."

"But I'm not hungry."

He kisses me on my cheek. "Well it'll be here when you get hungry."

I'm afraid to fall asleep again. I don't want to go back there. Can a person die from sleeplessness? I am willing to try. I never want to sleep again.

Chapter Three

I wake with a start. I fell asleep again without knowing it. No nightmare. No dreams at all. It was a glorious, dreamless sleep. Logan's body is entwined with mine. I have no idea what time it is, and I don't care. I'm home. My mother is safe, and Logan is by my side. Though, once he finds out what I went through over the last year, I wonder how many sleeps I can expect him to hold me through.

With my free arm, I shift myself and roll over so I'm facing him. Logan Wright. I used to joke that we'd see one day if he was, in fact, Mr. Right.

We were going on our second year of dating when I was taken. Logan and I met at USC. He was a film student and needed a blonde actress who didn't require payment for a short he was filming. Through mutual friends, the news traveled over to me at my performing arts college, and I jumped at the opportunity. He takes filmmaking very seriously. He was all business when we met, but I was immediately attracted to him. When I first saw him, I thought he was another actor with his clear blue eyes, dark brown hair, and tall, athletic build.

Having so much in common, we easily fell into dating. He isn't from L.A. like me. He's from Denver. But he was born to live by the ocean. Our courtship wouldn't be called a fairy tale, but I always loved that there was no competition between us. We both only wanted the best for each other. Before I was taken we had even begun discussing a future together. He was getting ready to graduate from USC, and I only had one year left. He was already accepted into NYU's prestigious graduate screenwriting program, and I planned on moving to New York as well—so we naturally began speaking about the idea of marriage. We both decided that we would wait to become more serious after college.

Most guys would run for the hills from a girl who believes in abstinence, but not Logan. He always felt the same way about it as me. "Too much instant gratification in the world and not enough sacrifice," he would say, especially when we would get cornered by some of our less understanding college friends who thought we were insane prudes. So the odds of meeting a guy who was into film and the arts and wanted to wait until he got married to have sex...I thought we were perfect for each other. It felt like fate to have found my *Mr. Right.*

With one hand, I brush his brown hair from his face. It's longer than I remember. He is sleeping so peacefully, like an angel. I wish we could stay just like this. In this moment, he most likely still loves me. Right now, he is happy about my unexpected return. Once he wakes up, he will learn I'm not the pure love of his life that I was before I was taken. I love him so much, but I fear that my love won't be enough. He is beautiful with his fair skin and soft, full lips. I wonder briefly if our kids would be brunettes like him, or blonde like me. I'm sure now I will never know.

Logan's eyes open and a sweet smile crosses his face. "Hey."

"Hey." I smile back at him. I can pretend for now that everything between us is okay and that the last year did not happen.

He stretches. "You okay? Any more bad dreams?"

"Nope. Not with you around." I give him a smile that is equal parts gratitude and relief.

"Good." He plants a kiss on my cheek. "Are you hungry yet?" He jumps out of my bed.

It's in this moment that I already know something is wrong. He hasn't questioned me about where I've been. *He already knows.* My mother let the cat out of the bag. "Logan. Can I ask you a question?" I come up onto my knees.

"Anything." He sits on the edge of the bed.

"Did my mother tell you what happened to me and where I've been this whole time?" I almost don't want to know the answer, but I have to know how to proceed with him. I'm tense and nervous bubbles fill my stomach as I await his answer.

He clears his throat. "She told me everything you told her. What you told the police."

"And?" I let the word drag out.

His brows furrow with confusion. "And what, Brinley?"

"You're still here?" I ask, my brows matching his.

He leans forward, takes my hand, and pulls me closer to him. "Listen..."

I can't bring myself to look at him. Fear of the words is causing my skin to crawl and my heart to race.

"I need you to look at me." He guides my chin gently with his hand toward him. I drag my eyes to his reluctantly, doing what I can to hide the hope in them.

"When your mother told me what you had to endure, I wanted blood. I still want nothing more than for someone to pay for what happened to you. But, Brinley, not you. You shouldn't have to pay. You have suffered enough. I loved you before you were taken. Nothing has changed."

I can't stop the waterfall that springs from my eyes.

"Do you want to talk about it?" he asks me.

I shake my head no.

"Then we won't talk about it." Logan wraps me in his strong embrace.

I wipe my eyes, nodding my head in agreement. "I just want to forget about everything. I know that I'll never be that lucky." I pull out of his embrace. I do my best to clean my face up with my quilt and I force a smile.

"I'd rather hear about you. I missed you so much, Logan. Tell me what I missed," I ask, wiping my eyes again, this time with the back of my hand.

I'm sure this is not what he really wants to talk about. How could he not want me to tell him all about the last year of my life? I am thankful to him for giving me some time. He loves me enough to give me what I need right now.

"Well, I graduated last May. My final film did very well. So well, in fact, that I landed a job with Bluest Moon Productions. I'm in the editing room, but it's all good. I want to learn every aspect of the filming process." He sighs, rubbing my back.

"Keep talking," I say because the silence is deafening. "Tell me more about working for a big film company. I'm so proud of you." *I am.* He has stayed focused on his dreams. But more than that, I'm happy to keep the conversation off of me. It keeps me out of my head. I know that I will have to talk about things eventually, but I just got home. I have forever to face what I will never forget.

"It's amazing, babe. Everything I ever wanted. I'm learning so much."

I'm a little surprised that Logan is this happy. We always planned to leave L.A. and head to New York together. New York was as much his dream as it was mine. We had it all planned out. He would go immediately following graduation and I would follow him a year later when I graduated. *If,* of course, I was accepted into Juilliard. It is now my belief that we are not the only ones in charge of our destinies, no matter how much as we plan our lives out. If we were, the last year of my life would never have happened. Being home now feels like waking up from a coma or being abducted by aliens for a year, only to be dropped out of the sky and back into my normal life. It feels familiar and strange at the same time. I missed an entire year of Logan's life. I have questions. *Why no NYU? Does he have a girlfriend?*

"What is it, Brin?" he asks.

"Nothing," I lie. I don't want to ask because I'm not sure I want the answer.

"You can ask or tell me anything. Just talk to me, please."

"It's just..." I look at him briefly and then away. "Getting on with Bluest Moon Productions is an amazing accomplishment, but what about your dream to go to NYU?"

He is silent as he stares into my eyes. "I couldn't go."

"Why? You were already accepted. What happened?"

"Some psycho kidnapped my girl off the fucking street, and everything in my life changed."

I drop my head to my lap. My tears fall with ease. I hear the anger in his voice.

"I'm sorry, babe. I know you're not ready to talk about what happened. Just know that I couldn't leave. I felt like as long as I stayed here, you would find your way back to me...you would come home. I was lost without you, and since New York was our dream, I just couldn't do it." He rubs my back.

"I thought about you every day, every minute," I cry out. "Thinking about you was the only thing that kept me strong, but, honestly, it also scared me to death." I cry harder. He pulls me back into his arms. "I was worried that you would find someone else. Or worse, that if I did make it out of there, you wouldn't want me anymore because of the things that were done to me."

He pulls me up and is gentle at the task of turning my face to his. "Brinley. There is only you. There will only ever be you for me. I will never stop loving you." Tears leak from his red-rimmed eyes as he weeps for me. "I love you."

"I love you ,too."

He continues. "No amount of time, no kidnapping, or rapist assholes will change that," he promises me.

Hearing the word "rapist" is like being slapped in the face. It accurately describes what I went through, but the use of that word also confuses me, because in spite of everything that happened to me, I was treated very well for the most part. *We will see if his promises hold true. I still don't know how much crazy I brought back with me.* After a year, I am no doubt changed, and only time will tell how and how much.

For now I can revel in the knowledge that, in this moment, he loves me.

Continue Reading Weeping Violet

AFTERWORD

Did you love Eclipsed Sunshine? Be sure to review it on Amazon and let other romance readers know what you thought!

💋 Dionne

MAILING LIST

Did you enjoy Eclipsed Sunshine be sure to join my mailing list and get the inside scoop on new releases, and have access to unreleased short stories about the characters you love!

D.W. MARSHALL'S DARK HEARTS

Want to talk with other romance lovers? Join my Facebook Group, D.W. Marshall's Dark Hearts.

ACKNOWLEDGMENTS

My wonderful cheer squad of friends and family that keep me excited and encourage me to keep going: Mom, whose vision of me at the finish line is a constant motivation. My sister-cousin Jamie who is one of the most positive people I know. Renee for your constant and valued friendship, you are a sister to me. Dolly, for letting me run my mouth and just being a great listener. My Girly Pop's, I just love you guys so much. My boys, Spencer and Jacksen for being a source of motivation for me. I won't give up my dream and I hope my determination teaches you to never give up yours. My Uncle Larry and Aunt Debbie for your constant support and encouragement. And a most special thanks to my husband. You are my gold medal, my Oscar, my Emmy. Your hard work inspires me and your love and support continues to drive me.

To my fans. Oh my goodness, I still can't believe I have those. Thank you for the messages and inspiring words. The fact that you love my work is a big reason I keep going. To my blossoming beta reader team, thank you so much for the love and support.

To my publishing team: The Danielles, Danielle Acee and Danylle Salinas, you two are the toughest editors I have ever met, and Danielle you assassinate my words and challenge me to write better. Thank you for the work you do as my Author Assistants. My cover artist, Heidi thank you for creating beautiful covers.

ABOUT THE AUTHOR

D.W. Marshall is a graduate of Tuskegee University. She is a native of California, but grew up in Las Vegas. If you opened her purse you'd find too many pens for one person, lip balm, and the dreaded receipts that never seem to go away.

D.W. loves to read dark *and* sweet romance, fantasy, YA, thrillers, and lives in Las Vegas with her husband, two sons, niece, and her one-eyed Bichon, named Sadie.

www.dwmarshallbooks.com

ALSO BY D.W. MARSHALL

The Seven Chambers Series

Stolen Flame

Weeping Violet

Shattered Sapphire

Poisoned Ivy

Eclipsed Sunshine

Cruel Obsessions Series

Twisted Soul

Coming Soon Twisted Heart

The Men of the Seven Chambers Series

Dominic

The Escorts Series

Keep up with D.W. Marshall

Made in the USA
Coppell, TX
18 February 2024

29143237R00148